"I'm trying to offer you some advice."

Gordon cleared his throat uneasily. "Vicky, it's difficult to tell you this...."

Vicky's face sobered suddenly. "I believe you're trying to warn me about something?"

"Yes," his voice rushed, "if you'll listen."

"Don't worry yourself about Nik and me," Vicky said tautly. "He's been good to me, but that's all. I don't imagine he's going to fall in love with me."

"Nik might be cosmopolitan," Gordon said tersely, "but he has strong prejudices. Nik doesn't take women seriously. I'll give Nik his due; he never asks for credentials, but marriage would be something entirely different, and I wouldn't like to see you hurt."

"There's nothing between Nik and myself," Vicky said, feeling suddenly numb.

MARGARET PARGETER

the demetrious line

Harlequin Books

TORONTO • NEW YORK • LONDON
AMSTERDAM • PARIS • SYDNEY • HAMBURG
STOCKHOLM • ATHENS • TOKYO • MILAN

Harlequin Presents first edition August 1983
ISBN 0-373-10620-3

Original hardcover edition published in 1983
by Mills & Boon Limited

Printed in U.S.A.

CHAPTER ONE

THE personnel officer smiled at the fair, slender girl in front of him and said smoothly, 'It's the chance of a lifetime, Miss Brown, as I'm sure you realise.'

Vicky Brown nodded uncertainly, too disconcerted by what she had just heard to be able to find her voice immediately. It might be the chance of a lifetime, as Derek Wilmot pointed out, but did she want to take it? Nicholas Demetrious—she had heard him referred to by one of his chief executives talking to Mr Hastings as Nik—was head of the vast organisation she worked for and in need of a secretary, but what made Derek think her qualifications were good enough for such a position? As she had received an excellent training, she supposed they would be. It was her ability to cope with the man himself which she doubted. Only once had she caught a brief glimpse of him during the three years she had been here, but his reputation as being difficult to please was well known. She would rather stay with Mr Hastings, who might be middle-aged and wholly predictable, but at least she knew where she was with him and he had always been kind to her.

Derek Wilmot watched the conflicting emotions chasing over Vicky's small, expressive face sympathetic-ally. 'Quite taken your breath away, hasn't it?'

Again Vicky nodded. Making an almost visible effort, she managed to ask dazedly, 'But why me?'

Derek shrugged. 'That's a question I really can't answer.' He grinned suddenly, teasingly. 'You're a very sweet young thing, but I hardly imagine it will be for that reason. I only know he's heard you're very efficient.'

'As P.A. to Mr Hastings,' Vicky said broodingly,

taking no notice of Derek's teasing which, she suspected, was meant to be more reassuring than flattering.

'Mr Hastings is no fool,' said Derek, more reprovingly. 'He wouldn't keep you if you weren't good at your job.'

'Which doesn't mean I'd be at all suitable for Mr Demetrious.'

'He's waiting to see you, anyway.' Derek didn't seem inclined to argue.

Vicky got reluctantly to her feet. 'He can't expect to find anyone as good as Miss Devlin.'

'Unfortunately Miss Devlin is now permanently in Athens.'

'She used to travel with him.'

'Apparently this doesn't suit Mr Demetrious any more.'

'It does seem rather strange,' Vicky frowned.

'Vicky, please!' Derek growled appealingly. 'Could you possibly stop wondering about something which I'm sure needn't concern you, and just go! Mr Demetrious isn't renowned for his patience and I did promise you'd be with him——' he consulted his watch, 'oh, no!' he exclaimed, 'three minutes ago!'

Vicky fled, although her legs felt so shaky she found it impossible to move as swiftly as she usually did. Her ability to think clearly wasn't so good either. She wanted to stay cool but couldn't prevent the thoughts churning through her head from making her angry. Shouldn't Mr Demetrious have discovered if she wanted to work for him first before sending for her without warning like this? He might be head of a business empire but that surely didn't mean he was free to disregard the feelings and inclinations of his staff. Or was this how such empires were built, by trampling roughshod over the feelings of others? She liked working for Mr Hastings, who was happily married and could keep his hands to himself. She enjoyed their ability to work well together, as well as their mutual respect. Had it been anyone else but Mr Demetrious she would have refused to even think of a move!

The girl she was presumably being interviewed to replace told her to go straight in, that Mr Demetrious was expecting her. As she was distraught and had obviously been crying, Vicky's nervousness grew. If someone several years older and therefore more experienced could be reduced to this, what chance did she stand?

Drawing a calming breath, she knocked with more apparent confidence than she felt on the door the girl had indicated before opening it gingerly. She didn't look up until she had stepped inside and closed it again.

When she did, and met the intent stare of a pair of narrowed grey eyes, a sense of shock ran distinctly through her. The one glimpse she had caught of Nik Demetrious had done little to prepare her for the actual reality. He was sitting at his desk, and she was startled to see the remoteness of his regard change suddenly to cold anger.

Thinking it must be because she had kept him waiting, Vicky forced herself to apologise. 'I'm sorry I'm late, Mr Demetrious.'

'I'm afraid I didn't give you much time,' he surprised her by noting quite cordially, making her believe she must have imagined the anger in his face. 'Do come in and sit down—Miss Brown, isn't it? I want to talk to you.'

He didn't appear in a hurry to begin. As Vicky obeyed him rather nervously, he continued appraising her silently until her own eyes began a little exploring of their own. For a moment she forgot to hide her curiosity as she hazarded a guess as to his height. He must be well over six foot, while the breadth of his shoulders suggested a strength above average. He was dark, his features rugged and full of vitality, his skin deeply tanned. Beneath the jacket of the fine grey suit which clothed his lean body so attractively, he was wearing a pristine white shirt. She noticed the immaculate cuffs, the glint of a gold watch, a sprinkling of dark hair over the backs of well kept hands.

Vicky swallowed, briefly forgetting she was staring. She mightn't have met Nicholas Demetrious before, but she was familiar with his reputation. People liked to talk about the rich and famous, and when on top of this a man had brains and personality he couldn't avoid becoming a subject for gossip. Most of which had gone over Vicky's head, but, on a less personal level, she would always be interested in the firm she worked for. She did know Mr Demetrious was a man of brilliant intellect whose driving power had made the Demetrious shipping line and its various subsidiaries what it was today. It was the sheer, overall impact she hadn't been prepared for. Again she gulped, trying unconsciously to stir a reluctant memory. She had been told he was around thirty-seven and while unmarried was no hermit. This Vicky had no difficulty in believing. His mouth was hard but also sensuous, and betrayed that he liked his own way—and was used to having it.

Involuntarily, her heart beating a little faster with what she took to be fear, she found herself stumbling backwards, until his curt voice jerked her to a halt.

'I think you're going in the wrong direction, Miss Brown.'

Colouring and feeling a complete fool, Vicky sat down, wishing he would take his eyes off her long enough for her to compose herself. If he scrutinised all his potential secretaries as closely no wonder they were soon reduced to the mindless idiots he soon declared them to be!

'I didn't realise what I was doing,' she stammered.

'I particularly want someone who does,' he replied sarcastically.

The colour in Vicky's cheeks deepened and her hands clenched by her sides. It must be her own fault if he had decided she was as silly as any of the others, but if he imagined she would be as easily downtrodden he would soon learn his mistake!

Coolly she returned his bland stare. 'I don't know why you should think I might suit you, Mr Demetrious.'

His heavy lids lowered a little over glittering eyes. 'You have no desire to work for me. Is this what you're trying to say?'

Vicky blinked, trying desperately to hang on to her former coolness. She had been about to nod and agree politely, but something in the deadly smoothness of his manner warned her like a red flag. Why did all her protective senses scream that if she refused to work for him she would soon be without a job of any kind? No one could be dismissed without good reason, she argued with herself, but that other part of her remained unconvinced. This man, this Greek of reputedly mixed parentage, would never let a little thing like protocol stand in his way. And she definitely needed every penny of her salary, especially now she had the house to maintain.

Suddenly she decided to be frank. There must be a more tolerant side to him—if she could reach it. Her violet blue eyes widening anxiously, she tried to make him understand. 'Until a few minutes ago. Mr Demetrious, I had no idea you were even considering me as your personal secretary. I've been with your organisation since I left school and finished my training, working for Mr Hastings. I don't really want to leave him.'

'Why not?'

Vicky had no difficulty in answering this time. 'We get on so well together.'

'In the office?'

She frowned, immediately disquieted by the suave insinuation in his voice. She was sure she must be wrong, but she had to find out.

'Mr Hastings isn't my boy-friend, if that's what you're implying. You mightn't know it, but he's a happily married man.'

'When has that ever stopped you? I'm talking generally, of course,' he added coolly.

Even that's not excusable! she wanted to retort, but again a hint of caution kept her silent. Mr Demetrious was insufferable, but, she reminded herself bitterly, it might be disastrous to tell him. What wouldn't she give though to be in his shoes for a change, to hold the whip hand and be able to state in no uncertain terms that, even after a mere ten minutes, she found him impossible! That she would rather die than have anything more to do with him!

Rather shocked at the vehemence of her feelings, when she was so rarely angry as a rule, she reiterated stiffly, 'I can assure you, Mr Demetrious, there's nothing at all like that between Mr Hastings and me.' Because she was so busy groping with confusion and his sceptical brows goaded her irrationally, she challenged him idiotically, 'If you don't believe me why not ask Mr Hastings? I assure you he finds it difficult enough on his salary to keep his wife and family without adding a girl-friend to the list of his expenses. He couldn't afford me.'

His eyes glinted. 'It would obviously take a richer man to do that, Miss Brown.'

Uncomfortably Vicky bit her lip, almost too startled to feel embarrassed. She had never had an interview like this before, and why did she have a suspicion that there was more behind it than was immediately apparent? What could there be, for heaven's sake? she thought impatiently, mentally cursing the kink of intuition she always seemed to have plaguing her. Conversation had a habit of straying from the main issue, perhaps that was half the charm of it, and, if she suspected Mr Demetrious of veiled insults, nothing had actually been discussed but her career.

'There aren't enough rich men to go round, Mr

Demetrious,' she replied primly. 'But I'm sure you didn't bring me here to talk about my matrimonial prospects.'

'I wasn't aware I'd got as far as that,' he murmured, in the smooth, velvety voice which made her shiver but which she suspected could as swiftly cut a girl in two if she wasn't careful. 'However,' he confessed, after a faint pause, 'I'll admit it was on my mind. I don't want to waste my time engaging a girl about to be married. I like my secretary to concentrate on me, rather than another man.'

'I could have a boy-friend,' Vicky was stung to retort sharply.

'I imagine you have several.'

Vicky had to restrain herself from getting up and walking out. His voice was level, his face almost expressionless, yet she had a distinct feeling he was getting at her. She was suddenly conscious of a surge of some kind of antagonism between them and frowned unhappily. If they reacted to each other like this already, how would it be if they were together continually?

'As it happens,' she said coldly, 'I have neither a boy-friend nor fiancé, at the moment.'

'Ah,' he murmured obliquely, 'an unfortunate experience?'

'You could say,' she replied, without feeling it necessary to explain that the unfortunate experience in her life had been her stepmother.

'People frequently deserve their unhappiness,' he remarked curtly. 'They act with often criminal thoughtlessness, then expect to escape the inevitable repercussions.'

He would make an excellent judge, Vicky thought sourly, feeling more like a prisoner about to be sentenced every minute. She was driven to observe coolly, 'If I had been about to be married, it's not unknown for a married woman to work.'

'If you were my wife you wouldn't,' he stated calmly.

'In Greece a husband usually makes sure his wife has more important things to think about.'

'Such as, Mr Demetrious?' she asked demurely, but with a brashness she hadn't known she possessed.

'The marriage bed and the cradle, Miss Brown,' he retorted sardonically, reaping a cynical revenge from the heightening colour in her cheeks.

Well, she had asked for that, she supposed. Briefly she closed her eyes so he wouldn't see her frustrated anger. It was a bit like taunting a tiger, she ought to have known better, but she would never have suspected him of having such old-fashioned ideas. It just proved that in some ways men were still pretty primitive, despite their veneer of civilisation. Cautiously she lifted heavy lashes to glance at Nik Demetrious again, but didn't dare suggest, as she was tempted to, that he only needed a club!

As she met his mocking gaze, he observed meaningfully, 'It appears you have no audible comment to make, Miss Brown?' When Vicky rather helplessly shook her head, he folded his arms on his desk, still watching her closely. 'So,' he emphasised, 'as you seem to be entirely heartfree, that's one problem disposed of.' Easing back slightly, he flicked cool eyes over a sheet of paper lying beside him. 'You've had your annual holiday, I see. Something else I consider an advantage.' Raising his head, he studied her again. 'You don't have much of a tan.'

Vicky thought she had a slight one, her usually pale skin was faintly golden. It must look fairly insipid, she realised, to a man used to people tanned to a much deeper brown, but he and his friends probably spent months in the sun instead of only a couple of weeks. And she had gone to Corfu to improve her knowledge of the language, more than anything else. If she had known then what she knew now, she might have stayed at home, for the money she had spent would have come in useful. Still, she had loved every minute of it.

'Where did you go?'

Vicky almost jumped as Nik Demetrious broke through her thoughts abruptly. Why should he be interested in where his employees spent their well-earned break? 'Corfu,' she replied quickly, the memory of it still able to bring a warm glow to her face. 'The weather was beautiful.'

'Enjoyed yourself, did you?'

This time Vicky couldn't possibly mistake the glint of cold derision in his eyes, and she wondered what she had done to earn it. She was certain they had never met before and he knew nothing about her apart from what was on her official record. He might have a few more relevant facts jotted down on the memo he occasionally consulted, but she had nothing to be ashamed of. She mustn't allow a foolish feeling of apprehension to drive her into imagining things which probably didn't exist.

Pulling herself together, she shrugged. 'Yes, I had a good time. Corfu is a pleasant place and the people are very kind.'

'I'm sure they are.'

For no reason she could think of she flushed and hated the way his glance sharpened as it pierced her hot cheeks. 'I expect you know the island well?'

'Well enough,' he grunted.

'But you don't live there.'

'How did you know?' he asked curtly.

'I'm not sure,' Vicky truly wasn't, and she wished she had never mentioned it, but then he appeared to treat everything she said with the same puzzling suspicion. 'I must have heard it from someone in the office,' she said hastily.

'Indeed?' His highly intelligent brows lifted. 'I rather believe I'm getting a very quick-witted secretary.'

What did he mean by that! Anxiously Vicky fell silent as he regarded her steadily. By now he must be familiar with every inch of her, and she was curious as to what he could be looking for. He couldn't be interested in a

beauty she didn't possess. Frowning, she discounted
pale hair, blue eyes and a skin like rose petals. She
could only conclude that he was deliberately goading
her and studying her reactions in an effort to discover if
she would be able to cope with his uncertain temper any
better than the other girls he had employed.

There was a brief pause while she tried not to notice
how hard his mouth had gone and was relieved when
his glance released her to flick downwards again.

'I see you speak several languages, Miss Brown?'

'German and French,' she agreed, feeling suddenly
on safer ground. 'I do have a smattering of Greek and
Italian which I'm trying to improve.'

'Good,' he rubbed a thoughtful hand round his
aggressive chin. 'I travel a lot, sometimes you might
have to come with me.'

Vicky was aware, despite her reluctance to work for
him, of a faint excitement. She had never travelled
with her boss before, and she wondered what it would
be like. Most probably he would work her so hard she
would never get the chance to see anything. Having
succeeded in squelching a rather premature exuberance,
she noted coolly, 'As Miss Devlin did?'

He smiled slightly, as though he was well aware of
the general curiosity regarding Miss Devlin. To Vicky's
surprise he explained, 'Miss Devlin suffers from a
rheumatic condition which has progressively worsened.
She hopes, we both hope, that a long spell in a warm,
dry climate will cure her.'

So her employment here might only be temporary.
Vicky was surprised by a twinge of disappointment as
she asked anxiously. 'If—I mean when Miss Devlin
returns, will I be able to go back to Mr Hastings?'

'Probably,' the broad shoulders lifted indifferently,
'but I don't think we need worry about that just now. I
suggest you come to me on a month's trial, Miss
Brown, then we shall see. If you prove satisfactory, I
might even be willing to let Miss Devlin retire.'

Was he dangling a carrot in front of a donkey? Vicky had a horrible feeling she might be wise to view such magnanimity in this light. Why did something continue to warn her she might live to regret accepting any offer this man made? Yet she was trapped, wasn't she? for she must have a job and the salary it paid. And while working for Nik Demetrious wouldn't be easy, surely, as Derek had said, it must be the chance of a lifetime?

Quickly Vicky thanked him, before she lost her nerve entirely and changed her mind. She turned her head, unconsciously seeking relief from his dark, implacable face as she rose slowly to her feet. The way in which he pushed his papers aside and relaxed in his chair appeared to indicate the interview was over, but Vicky was surprised to find she was still trembling. Nervously she glanced at him again, her hands sticky, her heart beating over-fast. 'Will that be all, Mr Demetrious?'

'Yes.' His eyes gleamed with a far from comforting satisfaction. 'You may begin on Monday.'

'Next week!'

'I hope there's nothing wrong with your hearing, Miss Brown?' he drawled smoothly. 'That's what I said.'

Vicky flinched before such sarcasm. 'It doesn't give Mr Hastings much time to find a replacement,' she faltered.

'Leave Hastings to me.'

Boiling slightly with both anger and apprehension, she was tempted, as she went out, to slam the door. Her delicate fingers curled round the handle with a violence quite foreign to her nature for several seconds while she struggled for control. She would have love to have slammed it until it jerked on its hinges, but somehow she was afraid to. Despising herself, she felt like a spider caught in a silken web, unable to break free. It should be easy—just a little willpower, she told herself fiercely, but already she was dominated by the strength of Nik Demetrious's unyielding personality. It might be futile trying to escape at this late hour, for she suspected that while the web he spun round a woman might have a certain silken charm, it might also be as strong as steel!

It was late when Vicky got home that evening and she felt unusually exhausted. For all her extremely delicate appearance, she had an amazing reserve of energy and vitality which proved invaluable in times of crisis. This afternoon mightn't have amounted to exactly that, but she did seem to have completed several days' work in as many hours.

Mr Hastings hadn't said much about her promotion, as he had called it, but she knew he was sorry she was leaving him. He had asked her to check on several items which had been scheduled for later in the month and to get in touch with Derek Wilmot about someone to replace her. Derek hadn't been available immediately and when she did find him he could only promise to do his best at such short notice.

Letting herself into the house, Vicky found a note on the hall table from Mrs Younger, who lived next door. Mrs Younger, who had always been like a mother to her as well as a neighbour, said she had left a pie for Vicky's supper in the fridge. Gratefully, for she was hungry, Vicky checked. The pie looked so appetising she was tempted to eat it straight away, but decided she'd better have a shower first. It had been a hot day, the air was still warm and her clothes, after a mad scramble on the tube, were damp with perspiration.

The long journey from the shipping offices home was tedious. Sometimes she regretted giving up the room near her job where she had lived for the past three years. She had only been back here a month and often it seemed longer.

Wryly she glanced around as she dropped the light waterproof she usually carried on the kitchen table and ran upstairs. The house was really much too big for her, but she was reluctant to sell it. So far she hadn't thought about it seriously, as she still found it difficult to believe it was hers at last. Daily she expected her stepmother to arrive, demanding it back, although legally, because of the terms of the will, she probably couldn't.

As Vicky showered she wondered where her stepmother was. There had been nothing since that one letter, along with the house key, had been pushed through Vicky's letter-box. In it Vera had merely stated that she had married a man rich enough to give her everything she wanted and was handing over the property. Vicky would not have wished for an invitation to the wedding, but she was surprised when Vera didn't even say who the man was. She hadn't even indicated whether she would be living in England or abroad.

Vicky wasn't really curious as to who Vera had married, but she would like to have known where she was living. She found it very difficult to relax, feeling Vera might be almost breathing over her shoulder. It made her unhappy and uneasy, even yet, for all she had seen practically nothing of her stepmother since her father had died, to contemplate the absolute failure of their relationship. Stepmothers weren't all alike, she knew, for several girls at work had them, mostly because of divorced parents. More often than not there developed an entirely amiable and workable arrangement, but Vera had never even tried. She had made it clear from the start that she just wasn't interested in her husband's twelve-year-old daughter. Unmercifully she had snubbed Vicky's tentative advances, until Vicky had learnt to keep out of her way, rather than risk upsetting her father.

Vera had wanted her out of the way permanently. Perhaps this was why she had voiced no real objection to Vicky's expensive boarding school. She had merely suggested a much cheaper one, but for once James Brown had put his foot down. As a child, Vicky had never been over-fond of school. She had been too shy and sensitive to mix well, but for the first time in her life she had been glad to go. The holidays had been miserable, though. Vicky still cringed when she recalled the days and weeks of Vera's cold disapproval and the evenings when frequently the house was filled with her gay, sophisticated friends, James, besotted with his beautiful wife until the end, had usually retired to his study, turning a blind eye and deaf ears to what was going on. He hadn't actually been a wealthy man, but he had been quite well off, and Vera had spent his money as if it was water. It had flowed out on expensive clothes, jewellery and holidays, and not least on huge quantities of wines and spirits which Vera had deemed absolutely necessary for successful entertaining.

Vicky had mercifully forgotten a lot, but the night she found Vera and one of her lovers in a spare bedroom remained imprinted indelibly on her memory. Whenever Vera gave a party, guests overflowed all over the house, and Vicky, because she hated them and like her father refused to attend, used to lock herself in her room. If she hadn't been so sensitive she might have sat with her father, but she had wanted to spare him the embarrassment, as Vera was one of the subjects they never discussed. If they spent the evening apart it was easier to pretend, next morning, that the party had never happened.

On this particular evening the top floor where Vicky slept had been quiet, so quiet in fact that when she heard a peculiar scuffle in the next room she thought the old family dog must have shut himself in. Being nearly blind, he didn't go out very much, but often got lost, even in the house. Scrambling out of bed, Vicky had gone smiling to rescue him, and stumbled across Vera and her boy-friend instead.

Vicky, at eighteen, had realised what Vera was like long ago, but she had been completely shocked by the scene which met her eyes as she had opened the door. But instead of being similarly dismayed by her unexpected entrance, the couple on the bed hadn't even attempted to cover themselves up. They had merely laughed at the dawning horror on her face and invited her jeeringly to join them.

Wholly nauseated, Vicky had flown back to her room, Vera's shrill, taunting laughter still ringing in her ears. She had vowed there and then that she would leave as soon as she could find somewhere to live. She didn't want to leave her father, nor did she wish to hurt him by telling him the truth, but if she was diplomatic she was sure he would understand. The next day, however, before she could consult him, he had been taken ill and suddenly died. The doctor had diagnosed a severe stroke which Vicky was secretly convinced had been brought on by worry and a broken heart. She hadn't said anything, it had been too late for words, anyway, but immediately after the funeral she had walked out.

She had found herself a room and settled down, fiercely glad that she had a job and could afford to be independent. The only contact she kept up in the street where she had been born was with Mrs Younger, and then she either met her somewhere or phoned her. She had hoped never to see Vera again and would never risk running in to her.

After several months, while Vicky was almost convinced that the disillusionment she had suffered at home hadn't permanently scarred her, it did seem to have put her off men for good. She didn't seem able to enter into a more than friendly relationship with them. This puzzled her, for, logically, she believed her disgust should have been more with her stepmother than with the opposite sex. She could only imagine that the repercussions of the shock she had endured had left something slightly twisted in her psychologically. Once she had allowed a boy she had been friendly with to kiss her and had felt so sick afterwards she had to push him away. She accepted now that it was something she might have to put up with all her life and there might be nothing much she could do about it. Knowing this, she kept men at a distance, although she realised they frequently looked at her with interest.

She tried to play fair in other ways too, doing her best not to attract them—hence her tightly screwed up hair and neat but floppy clothes. Recalling a faintly incredulous flicker in Nik Demetrious's dark eyes when once she had caught him glancing at her, she smiled slightly. At least she could almost guarantee there would be no problems with her new boss. She could imagine the type of woman he made passes at, and they wouldn't look at all like Vicky Brown!

That had been another of Vera's pet hates, the name Brown.

'I'm going to change it as soon as possible,' she had informed Vicky cruelly, before her father was even buried. 'It's a laugh!'

'You must have realised before you married him,' Vicky had replied wearily.

'Well, I've had enough!' Vera had returned sharply. 'And that goes for you, too. You can go as quickly as you like, and good riddance to you. I don't want to see your sanctimonious little face round here any more, with its holier-than-thou expression! You will know James left everything to me, of course.'

It had been a shock to Vera to discover eventually just how little money she had been left. Her husband's account had been practically empty, and while the house hadn't been mortgaged she had been livid to find she couldn't sell it. And if she married again it was to go to Vicky.

Vicky had been grateful to her father, but hadn't attached much importance to it. She had fully expected Vera to find a way round such a clause, and had been astonished, a few weeks ago, to receive the key. Mrs Younger could throw no light on the mystery either. She only knew that Vera had been on holiday in Greece and got herself into a spot of bother. Mrs Younger couldn't say exactly what it was, Vera hadn't been very explicit, but reading between the lines Mrs Younger had gathered that Vera had become somewhat seriously involved with one man but was going to marry another.

'She made a joke of it, dear,' Mrs Younger said dryly, 'but I think she was frightened of something, otherwise I don't believe she would have told me anything.'

Vicky didn't think so either, for there had been no love lost between Vera and their next-door neighbour. But as for Vera being in any serious trouble, Vicky doubted it. Vera was, after all, thirty-three, and too much of an expert at playing one man off against another not to know exactly what she was doing.

Switching off the shower, which was now running almost cold, Vicky dried herself hastily and flung on a pair of old jeans and a shirt without paying much attention to her general appearance. Putting her stepmother firmly from her mind, she returned to the kitchen to have her supper. Then she went to find Mrs Younger to thank her for the pie.

It wasn't until three weeks later that Vicky paused one evening to really look at herself. She couldn't remember doing this since she had left home three years ago, and she was surprised to find she didn't seem to have changed much. Her general image had changed, though, she decided with a wry grimace. She looked far more prim and proper than she had looked then. Surveying her tightly screwed up hair, she wondered curiously if this could be responsible for her rather spinsterish appearance. Experimentally she took out the pins, letting it fall free about her small face.

The difference it made was remarkable. Usually she brushed it and knotted it, then pinned it back without a glance, apart from making sure it was tidy. Now she was faintly entranced to see how it appeared not to have suffered from such ruthless treatment. It lay against her well shaped head, gleaming softly, like pale gold silk. Why hadn't she realised before that it was such a lovely colour? Her eyes left it to wander uncertainly over her fine-boned features, noting her delicate little nose and high cheekbones; her wide violet eyes and gold-tipped lashes. Was her mouth, she wondered, just a shade too generous?

Then she flushed, for despite being alone she felt selfconscious about studying any part of herself. And she could think of little to be gained by it, because there wasn't anything she could change very much. Her bust might be rather obvious, but it was firm and quite a good shape. She might diet, but then she would probably lose weight all over, and her waist and hips were already too slender. Vicky frowned, unaware that both her face and her figure were near perfect and she had no need to be so disparaging.

CHAPTER TWO

PURSING the mouth she had stared at so doubtfully, Vicky turned impatiently from the mirror, unfairly blaming Nik Demetrious for such foolish self-interest. It must be because his eyes went so frequently over her that she had suddenly become aware of herself as a woman. Yet, she rebuked herself, his stare was often abstracted; he could easily be thinking of something else.

Quietly she acknowledged that he hadn't turned out to be quite the dominating, ill-tempered boss she had expected. In fact there were times when he was quite charming, and certainly he was considerate. He might work all hours and frequently forget she was a girl and not a machine, but he always made up for it. Last night, for instance, he had taken her out for dinner, after they had finished, and insisted on driving her home afterwards.

The meal they shared had been quite an experience. Nik Demetrious had been flatteringly attentive and she had responded to him like a flower opening to the sun. She was still trying to control her quivering senses as he had drawn up outside her door. She had had a crazy notion, as his lids had come half down over glittering eyes and he leaned towards her, that he had been about to kiss her, when suddenly he had appeared to notice the size and location of the house.

His quick anger had startled her, and she had been rather angry herself when his head jerked up and he had asked abruptly how she came to be living in such a place.

She could only imagine he pigeonholed all clerical staff in to one-roomed flats! Her cheeks hot at such arrogance, she had replied more flippantly than she might otherwise have done, 'I was given it,' which, in a way, was the truth, but he had pushed her out of the car and roared off, without giving her a chance to explain.

The next morning at the office he made no reference to his burst of bad temper, and while Vicky was curious, as the day wore on she forgot about it.

Towards the end of the week she slept in one morning and was late. Hurrying to the office, she arrived breathless, fully expecting to feel the weight of Nik Demetrious's wrath again. He couldn't stand people who weren't on time, and she was near to tears with frustration when his assistant, Gordon Taylor, with whom he worked closely, told her that Nik had been ringing for the last ten minutes.

'He's on the warpath,' Gordon said dryly. 'You'd better watch out.'

So much for her month's trial! Vicky thought wretchedly, grabbing a pad before dashing in to present herself, realising she might be dismissed on the spot. She even felt grateful that Gordon had warned her as she braced herself to hear the fateful words.

Nik Demetrious did ask her rather sharply where she had been, but he cut short her humble apologies. 'I don't expect you to be perfect all the time, Miss Brown. I'm not inhuman.'

Why did she have a terrible feeling he was? As she stared at him, nerves leaping as he continued searching in his desk for something, she was suddenly sure he was furious and striving to hide it. He wouldn't normally be inclined to spare his employees' feelings, and she wondered why he was doing so now. To add to her confusion, when he raised his head it was to ask cordially if she would like some coffee before they began.

Vicky wasn't used to such consideration. It startled her, but she managed to murmur a few feverish words of appreciation, doubting if she would ever understand him.

She slipped out of her coat, getting rid of it unobtrusively, and sat in her chair, pen poised, waiting for him to begin. When he did, he dictated several letters at high speed, as if regretting his former leniency, scarcely giving her time to drink the coffee which arrived. Then he dictated and studied several reports, with Gordon always in the background ready to supply any missing details. The session was hectic, continuing without a pause until lunchtime. Before leaving for lunch, Nik Demetrious ordered Vicky to have the letters ready for him to sign when he got back and to be ready to accompany him to a board meeting.

Vicky went straight to her typewriter. The girl who might have helped her had already left for her lunch and Vicky knew better than to leave the letters until she returned.

'Shall I send for some sandwiches?' Gordon asked, sardonically eyeing the pile of work on his desk and dismissing his own chances of eating out as well.

'That would be lovely!' Vicky flashed him a smile of sheer gratitude which made him draw a sharp breath. 'The coffee was good this morning, but I missed breakfast.'

'You were lucky to get anything.' Gordon wrenched his eyes from her face to pick up the phone.

Impulsively Vicky almost asked if Mr Demetrious was always such a slave-driver, but in view of Gordon's loyalty she revised her question slightly. 'Does he always work so hard?'

'Yes,' Gordon replied shortly, sensing the slightest criticism and on the defensive immediately. As Vicky flushed unhappily, he relented slightly. 'He doesn't believe in sparing himself, you know. He never asks us to do more than he does himself.'

He rarely works through his lunch hour, though, Vicky thought angrily, remembering the call which had come in the middle of the morning. She knew it had been from a female and she suspected Nik was having lunch with her. It had been fairly obvious, and he'd said he would see her at one-thirty. A flicker of something she was reluctant to recognise as envy shot through Vicky as she thought of him with another girl.

'He—he has a lot of drive,' she agreed quickly, deploring her own weakness.

'Enough for ten,' Gordon made sure she realised.

His more approving glance encouraged her to voice her growing fears. 'I'm only here on a month's trial, he mightn't keep me.'

Gordon grinned, his monkey-like face crinkling. 'I shouldn't worry too much if I were you, darling. You've got qualities he values.'

'Such as?' she asked huskily.

'Why should I tell you?' he teased.

'I could use a bit of flattery,' she grinned back, not entirely hiding her anxious expression.

'Okay,' Gordon's smile faded, 'but I'd better be brief or we'll never get anything done. I guess you don't break down under stress, by this morning's work you've proved you can take it. You don't clock-watch either, and you can concentrate. You also have the ability to anticipate his needs. Shall I go on?'

'Oh,' exclaimed Vicky, feeling breathless, as if she had just recited it all herself, 'that will do to be going on with, I think.'

'I think you rather surprised us both, Miss Brown,' Gordon said contemplatively. 'I'll admit I was a bit bewildered when he decided on you. I guess his intuition must be better than mine.'

'That smacks of a back-handed compliment.' Vicky shot Gordon a dry glance as she removed the cover from her machine.

That evening, Nik Demetrious asked if she would mind working for an hour or two at his flat. He had some tapes there he wanted to use, and it was more private.

Wondering what could be more private than this

huge block of offices, with doorkeepers checking everyone who came near, Vicky gathered up her things and followed him meekly. Gordon would be there, although he said he would be leaving early to meet his mother off a plane from Italy.

'My manservant will provide you with dinner,' Nik Demetrious murmured softly as Gordon walked ahead of them to the lift. His slightly mocking tones told Vicky he was well aware that she was nervous of being alone with him. 'Dion,' he added, 'is a very good cook.'

Vicky was sure he would be. She couldn't imagine Mr Demetrious putting up with anything less than the best. Perhaps that was why he hadn't yet married? He might not have found a girl he considered good enough for him. As a flicker of scorn passed through Vicky's blue eyes, she bent her fair head for fear he should read her derisive thoughts. The next few days might be crucial; she had better not annoy him if she wanted to keep her job.

He had a penthouse suite in an expensive area. She was a little startled by the sheer luxury of it. While Dion spoke to him for a few moments, Gordon whispered that the manservant was always in attendance for when Nik was in the U.K. or any of his family visited.

'His grandmother lived in Greece but used to come often,' Gordon said soberly. 'She was English and very grande-dame, though entirely approachable. She died six months ago, and he still misses her.'

So Nik Demetrious wasn't wholly Greek. He had only a trace of accent when he was angry, but she had thought him too dark to have any English blood in his veins. Maybe his eyes might have provided a clue, as they were often as cool as the grey northern skies, and in many ways he was as English as any other man she had worked for.

Whatever his ancestry, his looks were impressive, Vicky admitted hollowly, not caring for the way her pulse beat unevenly as she watched him talking to Dion. He had a tall, powerful body and the sensuous mould of his mouth was far from cold. There was something about him that could bring a flush to her cheeks when he glanced at her in a certain way. He was unquestionably sexy in a hard, aggressive fashion, and she could no longer wonder at his popularity with women.

Since coming to work for him as his secretary, Vicky had begun scanning the newsprint daily for snippets of gossip about him which she had formerly despised. Apart from one picture of him escorting a famous model, she had seen nothing. She wouldn't have thought he was that discreet, and she frowned as she wondered just how many women he had taken out and made love to.

She couldn't really believe that the disturbing flicker of feeling which had seemed to shoot through her recently, whenever she thought of him with other women, was jealousy. It wasn't uncommon, she realised, for a secretary to be attracted to her boss, but she had worked among attractive men for years without feeling the slightest stir of her senses. While it mightn't be exciting, the emotionless cocoon she had lived in for the past four years was relatively comfortable and she would hate to think that anyone so remotely removed from her own humble circles as Nik Demetrious had the ability to shatter it. What she was experiencing could only be a touch of the kind of idolatry youngsters often felt for stars or famous people far removed from their own personal orbits. Whatever it was she felt for Nik Demetrious it would, she was sure, if she was careful, eventually work its way out of her system. She wasn't prepared to acknowledge that it was anything more than the mildest of infatuations.

They worked until almost nine when Gordon departed to go to the airport. He waved them a cheerful goodbye, a tall man in his early thirties, not handsome but possessing a lively, intelligent personality. When he had gone Nik Demetrious rang for dinner to be served, although Vicky assured him she would as soon go straight home.

'Nonsense,' he dismissed her protests authoritatively, 'you've had a long day. You can't possibly go back to an empty house and a probably empty larder.'

Not having enough energy left to fight him, she gave in and asked if she might wash her hands.

He showed her to a bedroom with a bathroom attached. 'Will this do? Miss Devlin often used it.'

He smiled at her and she thanked him shyly, her pulses fluttering. She was happier for knowing that Miss Devlin had come here, that it must be part of his normal routine to work here occasionally. It made her unconscious apprehension seem slightly ridiculous, but the relief she felt more than made up for her temporary embarrassment. Would she always feel threatened, she wondered, when alone with a man?

She heard the door click as Nik Demetrious went out and closed it behind him, and a faintly impatient sigh escaped her lips. Wasn't it time she stopped being so silly as to imagine she had any need to feel threatened as far as he was concerned? If he thought of her at all it would only be as an efficient cog in his business machinery. He could have no personal interest in her whatsoever!

She washed in the green and silver bathroom, the water cool against her hot face and hands. Her head ached, and in a moment of recklessness she sought relief by freeing her tightly coiled hair and arranging it in a looser style. She had no make-up with her apart from a lipstick, having left home that morning in such a hurry. Hoping it would distract Nik Demetrious's eyes from her otherwise bare face, she applied it over-generously.

With her hair falling about her shoulders, she didn't think she looked so very different, but he stared at her as she returned to the lounge. He was busy pouring drinks and his eyes were still narrowed as he placed one in her hands.

Suddenly his face was grim and she saw his nostrils flare in temper. 'So this is what you've been hiding?' he exclaimed.

Vicky stared at her drink as her heart began beating in nervous panic. Illogically she wondered if it was sherry. There was something in his voice which made her feel in urgent need of something to sustain her, but she had no head for anything stronger. Apprehensively she closed her eyes, tilting a fiery mouthful down her slender throat, managing to utter incomprehensibly as she choked. 'I'm afraid I don't understand.'

'I scarcely recognised you.' He waited, dark brows raised ironically until she recovered, but all traces of his confusing fury had gone.

She shivered, relief flooding her as his cold grey eyes warmed slightly again. 'Because of my hair, you mean?'

'Yes.' To her amazement his hand came out to lift a pale, silken strand of it. There was something deliberate in the way he did it which brought back her fading fear. 'It's a beautiful colour,' he observed coolly.

A different colour ran hotly under her creamy skin as she tugged quickly from him, feeling a sharp pain before he let her go. Had he meant to hurt? she wondered, blinking away a tear.

'Why do you wear it differently?' he asked, apparently not noticing how his roughness had brought tears to her eyes.

'I can work better when it's tidy,' she faltered, the flush on her face deepening as she realised this was only half the truth.

'Haven't you ever thought of having it cut short?'

'I thought men didn't care for short hair,' she was suddenly horrified to hear herself replying. It sounded so much like a flirtatious challenge that she wished the ground would open and swallow her up. What must he be thinking? He might never believe he had reduced her to such turmoil she scarcely knew what she was saying. She seemed no longer a cool, efficient secretary but a quivering, helpless woman.

His eyes were still intent on her. She had removed her jacket while they were working, because it had been warm, despite the air-conditioning, and the fine blouse she wore did little to hide the seductive curves of her slender figure. As she stiffened instinctively the slight tension which had been between them since the beginning tightened into something almost visible.

Her heart began to race as his glance ranged completely over her while the line of his strong mouth hardened. 'It all begins to add up,' he said grimly. 'And men being naturally fools . . .'

'What adds up, Mr Demetrious?' she broke in with a gasp. She wished fervently that he would stop talking in riddles she failed to comprehend.

Her urgent desire to know what was wrong was frustrated by Dion's knock, yet his announcement of dinner brought a welcome sense of relief. There appeared to have been a subtle shift in the relationship between Nik Demetrious and herself in the past half hour, but she had no idea what it was or how it had come about. Whatever it was it must be up to her to make sure he understood that her only ambition was to work for him, nothing more.

Was she sure there was nothing more? Clumsily Vicky placed her unfinished drink on the low table near her, her movements unusually unco-ordinated because of a fleeting sense of shock. She couldn't understand her own emotions, but she knew she had never been aware of them like this before. Nik's presence, however, to which she was reacting so strongly, wasn't giving her a chance to sort anything out. If only she could make some kind of endeavour to get things back on an even keel, perhaps she could ignore everything else.

But before she could speak he had taken her arm with a brief shake of his head which seemed to suggest he was no longer interested in what they had been discussing, 'Come along,' he said, politely guiding her to the dining-room. 'Dion won't thank us if the food he's prepared is ruined.'

Vicky never clearly remembered what Dion served them with that evening. Some of the food had a distinctly Greek flavour and it was all delicious, melting in her mouth. And with each course the wine was cool and potent. As the meal progressed, Nik Demetrious's former antagonism appeared to leave him and he was charming to her. And Vicky, because she was tired and failed to keep a check on how much she was drinking, found herself responding helplessly to his charm, unable to resist it.

He talked a little about Greece, but mostly in connection with the various aspects of his business. If Vicky's head hadn't been slightly dizzy from the amount of wine he pressed on her, she might have been surprised that he mentioned the size of his business empire several times, as if deliberately to impress her. Once such a thought did occur to her, but she shrugged it off. Men like Nik Demetrious didn't need to use words to impress, their track record more than did this for them.

He didn't usually spend so long in London, he said. More often he was in America or Athens, and he had a villa on one of the Greek islands which he didn't manage to visit often but which he considered was his real home.

'I built it myself, on the site of an old peasant's cottage.' His voice held a sudden coolness as he glanced at her. 'The peasant who had lived there was actually an ancestor of mine. Several distant members of my family still live on the island, though not near me.'

He didn't say which island it was, and she was about to enquire when he abruptly changed the subject.

Before she could ask her question he was asking one of his own.

'The house you are living in is large, is it not, Miss Brown. How long have you been living there?'

Vicky supposed that as he had talked about his own home he thought it only polite to show some interest in hers. Nevertheless, recalling his as yet unexplained anger on the evening he had taken her home after work, she was nervously wary. 'About a month,' she replied briefly.

He appeared to be waiting for her to go on, but she remained stubbornly silent. She was sure her family history would only bore him, and how could she tell him of the barren desert that had been her father's second marriage, about her stepmother's lovers? And the harrowing details of her father's will were surely too private to discuss with anyone.

'Isn't such a house too big for you?'

She glanced at him quickly as he eventually broke the uneasy silence, but his face was still kind. It encouraged her to confess, 'I have thought of selling it, but there are—well, unusual circumstances.'

'If it was a gift then it must be yours to do with as you like.'

So he hadn't forgotten. His mind was so rapier-sharp she might have known he wouldn't! Still reluctant to confide in him, she avoided his probing gaze. 'I—I'm rather afraid to dispose of something I've only just received.'

Because she wasn't looking directly at him, her glance fell on one of his hands resting on the table, and she was startled to see it suddenly clench until the knuckles turned white. Wondering how her rather negative statement could have disturbed him so much, she was equally surprised when he merely remarked quietly,

'You're a beautiful girl, why aren't you married?'

As his hand relaxed she judged that he had probably

been thinking of something else in between making polite conversation. Even so, she had no wish for him to know of the shock she had experienced years ago, which had isolated her from all thoughts of men and marriage. She could never explain how it had come about. It made her feel ill to think of it, even after so long. The coldness which usually enveloped her whenever she thought of Vera was reflected in her eyes as she replied with a flippancy she hoped defensively would deceive him,

'I have a better time not taking men seriously.'

'Don't you mind if they suffer?'

Although his tone might have matched her own, she had a feeling that, for some reason, her answer was important to him. 'People rarely experience the same degree of emotion,' she retorted, thinking more of Vera and her father.

He stared at her pale face, clearly unimpressed by her halting reply. 'And in your case you always make sure it's the man who cares most? Aren't you frightened you might one day meet a man who might break your heart for a change?'

'Perhaps ...' She was finding it difficult to concentrate. She felt too weary and confused to really know what she was saying, and Nik Demetrious's eyes were suddenly so disapproving she was certain she must have said something she shouldn't.

'You're quite without conscience, aren't you?'

She must have said the wrong thing! Her heart sank as she protested feebly, 'I should hope not, Mr Demetrious.'

'Never mind,' he muttered curtly. 'Why give ourselves indigestion? I brought you here this evening to work, not insult you. Please forgive me.'

She smiled at him softly, quite willing to forgive him anything if only he would be nice to her again. She was sure his mouth was beginning to relax when Dion came to tell them he had taken the coffee tray to the lounge.

Later, Nik Demetrious took her home himself, having dismissed his chauffeur earlier in the evening. This time, when they arrived at her door, he insisted on seeing her safely inside.

'Quite impressive,' he murmured, stepping into the hall behind her.

She nodded, trying to see it through his eyes. The furnishings, though shabby, were still good, but she was too tired to do more than glance round without a great deal of interest.

'I imagine you took everything over with the house?'

Again she nodded, surprised but not alarmed by his question. There must be thousands of houses like it in London, and she wondered what there could be about this one that was attracting his attention.

'Thank you for bringing me home, Mr Demetrious.' She thought of offering him coffee but decided against it as they had only just had some.

'It was the least I could do,' he said.

She smiled at him gravely, her wide blue eyes holding a look of sleepy innocence. 'It was very nice of you anyway.'

'Goodnight, Miss Brown.' After one harshly penetrating stare he turned abruptly and left her.

As she bolted the door behind him she heard the engine of his car rev sharply and he was gone. Why did something about the house appear to annoy him? A frown creased Vicky's smooth brow as she could find no answer. He was a strange man, she thought, gazing down on her trembling hands, quite sure she would never understand him.

When she heard from Gordon that Nik was going to New York for two weeks, a sigh of relief ran through her. While she would miss his drive and initiative, which was so much a part of him, his absence would give her the breathing space she felt she badly needed. If Nik Demetrious was away for a week or two it would give her a chance to sort out her feelings and get back to normal before he returned. She had no wish to fall in love with any man, because she knew she could never face the intimacy this must involve, and apart from this, wouldn't it be utterly foolish for a girl in her position to fall for a man like Nik Demetrious who, long ago, must have built up an impenetrable immunity against the female members of his staff.

Vicky's sigh of relief turned to one of despair when she learned that she was to go to New York with him. He told her himself, and she stared at him with a dismay he obviously found irritating.

'Come, Miss Brown,' he said curtly, 'you must know that a secretary to a man such as myself is sometimes expected to go abroad with him?'

'Yes,' she whispered.

Her nervousness appeared to irritate him even more. 'We discussed this.'

'Yes, of course,' she tried to speak coolly this time. 'I don't really mind.'

'It's very good of you, Miss Brown, to be so obliging,' he observed dryly, his eyes on her hair which was back in its old style.

She flushed. 'You haven't forgotten I'm here on a month's trial?'

'Which ends this week. No,' a thin smile formed on his hard mouth. 'I hadn't forgotten, far from it. I've decided to keep you on.'

For the past three weeks she had been hoping he would, so where was the happy relief she might have expected? Why did she only feel suddenly frightened?

'You want me to stay?' she murmured huskily, half praying he might change his mind.

'I do,' he confirmed smoothly, watching her face as she gazed at him, as if trying to read her confused expression. 'I find you surprisingly competent as a secretary. I'd like you to sign a contract to work for me for a year.'

Vicky hesitated, her heart thudding, every startled beat of it advising caution. 'Is that usual?'

'Miss Brown,' he said tersely, thrusting a sheet of paper towards her, to her amazement already prepared for her signature, 'I have no intention of arguing with you. Either you want this job and what it entails or you don't!'

Blindly Vicky found herself glancing over the printed form. There was quite a lot of it, but it seemed to say everything he said it would, and the terms quoted were extremely generous. More than she was ever likely to get elsewhere, and it was only for a year. She wasn't exactly signing her life away!

As she picked up a pen his face held a strange look of hard triumph, but he merely said quietly, 'When I find staff I can rely on I like to keep hold of them.'

She could understand that.

Glancing at her signature, he folded the form and placed it in his pocket. 'Gordon will see to everything you require for the trip,' he told her, on his way to keep an early appointment. 'Just be ready to leave at a moment's notice.'

Vicky was relieved that Gordon was coming too. 'I don't always,' he told her as they waited for their flight at the airport, 'but this is a big merger going through, meaning a lot of work. Nik's going to need me.'

Vicky was well aware of Gordon's usefulness. It was herself she still had doubts about. What she had heard of American secretaries wasn't exactly unimpressive. She feared she might show up badly by comparison and let both Mr Demetrious and Gordon down.

'All this might be strange to you, but you have to learn some time, you know,' Gordon was proffering his usually comforting advice. 'A little experience and you'll soon be as good as Miss Devlin, and she travelled with us a lot.'

Glancing at Nik's tall figure, as he talked to an official, Vicky shivered. 'It must take years . . .' she began.

'So what?' Gordon cut in. 'Just don't panic, Vicky.

You're young and intelligent and this morning you're looking very lovely. You have everything going for you. What more can you ask?'

Vicky knew he was right. She knew she had too little confidence in herself. Even Vera had often sneered at her about it, saying she was too self-effacing to be true. Everybody couldn't be wrong, Vicky reasoned soberly; even Nik Demetrious had signed her on, so to speak, for a year. Perhaps it was time she perked up and made the most of it.

The last few days had been so hectic she had scarcely had a moment to think. As well as her work in the office there had been lot of other things to do. Somehow, though, she had managed. In fact, she felt amazingly revitalised by all the extra activity. As Gordon had hinted, perhaps if she gave herself a chance she might be capable of far more than she had ever imagined.

Nik Demetrious had taken no interest in her personal preparations other than to tell her to pack one or two smarter outfits than she seemed to wear in London. He had reached into his desk for his cheque book, written a cheque, folded it, and when she had hesitated ordered her to take it. He had told her to take half a day off and have her hair done while she was at it.

'You don't come with me as you are,' he had said calmly, ruthlessly silencing her protests, his cool glance resting on her tortured head. 'I don't know who you're trying to impress with that hair style, but it certainly doesn't impress me!'

'I'm not trying to impress anyone,' she had replied, feeling curiously near to tears.

He had shrugged, not appearing to notice she was upset. 'Don't argue with me, Vicky, please.'

She hadn't had any breath left to after that. Not after he called her Vicky for the first time. She hadn't even noticed the slight flicker of derision in his eyes as she managed to thank him, being only aware of her heart thudding heavily in her breast.

It was Gordon who sat beside her on the plane. They travelled first class and she found it extremely comfortable. Gordon said that although he was based in London he did a lot of travelling and found it boring. It wasn't often he had a pretty girl to talk to.

Vicky was quite happy to talk to him and wished her eyes didn't search so frequently for a glimpse of Nik Demetrious. He had been hailed by a beautiful American woman as they boarded the plane and he seemed to be paying her a lot of attention. Gordon whispered that he thought it was someone Nik had known years ago and he was certain their meeting hadn't been prearranged.

'Something like this usually happens,' he grinned. 'That's why, on shorter journeys, we nearly always use Nik's private jet. Then we can work.'

Nik didn't appear not to be enjoying himself! Vicky watched him conversing with the woman by his side with a trace of envy, wondering what it must be like to be sitting next to him, the sole object of his attention. He was looking very self-assured and attractive in a superbly cut suit with a tight-fitting waistcoat. Vicky's soft mouth compressed as his companion spoke and his face softened as he laid a quick hand on her arm and bent forward to catch what she was saying. As he straightened again, as though conscious of her interest, he turned his head and his eyes locked directly into Vicky's.

A sense of shock rushed through her immediately, tying her stomach in knots and making her mouth dry. As their eyes met, she tried to but couldn't look away. As his glance transfixed her, she felt she was drowning in the dark, surging depth of an emotion that seemed to project from him and sweep right over her. There was nothing she could do about it. His grey gaze was long and steady on her face, and she saw his eyes harden as her breath caught and her heart began to race. Afterwards she was grateful that one of the air hostesses should have chosen that moment to pass between them. Otherwise she wasn't sure how she would have released herself from his dark, enigmatical gaze.

After this she made a special endeavour not to look at him but concentrated wholly on the pile of magazines he had surprisingly bought for her at the airport. It took her several minutes to stop trembling and much longer to make any sense of what she was reading. She couldn't explain even to herself what had happened to her in those few moments when she had looked into Nik's eyes and the world, for her at least, had seemed to stand still. It was something of a shock to feel her former apprehension dissolving before fears of quite a different nature. As she had gazed at Nik Demetrious, she had had an urgent desire to be closer to him, even to be held in his arms. And knowing she had felt like this, if only for a few seconds, terrified her. It stunned her that all the former barriers she had erected against men could so easily be swept away.

CHAPTER THREE

On arrival in New York, they were met by a chauffeur-driven limousine and driven swiftly to an apartment on the Upper East Side. Manhattan, Gordon had mentioned on the plane, was the city's central area and the smallest of its five boroughs.

'It has just about everything you've ever heard of,' he had grinned, 'Everything from Wall Street to Fifth Avenue, and the Empire State Building is there. You'll enjoy it, once you get used to it.'

If she ever got the chance to get used to it! Vicky thought wryly, hiding her disappointment as they moved through the streets so fast she scarcely caught more than a glimpse of anything. Her first impression was of a lot of people, noise and dirt.

At the apartment, Nik handed her over to his Greek housekeeper Obelia, who, with her husband Philo, looked after the place for him. Then he disappeared with Gordon, to do a few hours' work before dinner. He told Vicky he would see her then but wouldn't require her for anything until the next day.

Obelia, a woman in her forties, showed Vicky into a beautifully decorated and furnished bedroom. Vicky thanked her, her voice warm with appreciation.

'I'm glad you like it,' the woman smiled, then positively beamed when Vicky asked if she was any relation to Dion, in London. 'He is my husband's cousin. Did he send a message for us, do you know?'

Vicky was forced to confess that she had only met Dion once, but she was sure he wouldn't have forgotten them. 'I expect Mr Demetrious will be giving you all his news, when he has time,' she said.

'When he has time!' Obelia repeated with rueful laugh. 'He is a good man, is Mr Demetrious, but a workaholic, if there ever was one! What he needs is a wife. One day, I pray he will settle down with a woman his family approves of and she will teach him that there is more to life than making money!'

Vicky suspected Nik's life didn't consist entirely of work and perhaps Obelia was worrying unnecessarily, but Nik's personal affairs had nothing to do with her, and she got on with her unpacking. Obelia shook her head and departed when Vicky refused her help, murmuring something about preparing dinner.

When she had finished hanging her few things away, Vicky lay on her bed, surrendering wearily to the effects of travel and jet-lag. She hoped she wouldn't be around when Nik Demetrious married. It might be altogether too painful.

Obelia thoughtfully brought her a cup of coffee and, after drinking it, she dozed for an hour or two, until it was time to have a shower and dress for the evening meal. The apartment was very quiet, the sounds from outside muted. They might have been right out in the country rather than in the middle of a city.

During dinner Nik and Gordon talked mostly about business. Only occasionally did they include Vicky in their conversation, but she was content to listen. Listening was one of the best ways to learn, her father had always said, and even after a rest, she still felt too strangely tired to do anything else.

Sometimes, though, when Nik smiled at her, she felt the pull of his dark attraction and found herself coming alive again. Unhappily she wondered what she was going to do about it. We are frequently at the mercy of our emotions, how could she argue with that? How could she be wiser than those who had proved it over and over again? All she could do was to try and keep out of Nik's way when they weren't working. Secretly she hoped that Gordon

might help her in this by asking her out occasionally.

It soon became clear, however, in the days that
followed, that this was not to be. Gordon continued
being kind and considerate, but he had duties and
friends which didn't include her, and she often spent
long hours alone with Nik. Usually he went out early in
the morning, taking Gordon with him, but he
frequently returned by himself with a bulging briefcase.
He gave her notes to write up and tapes to transcribe,
and dictated letters when he wasn't on the telephone.
Vicky certainly couldn't complain she had nothing to
do, but it seemed to her that what she was doing here
was merely a continuation of the more or less routine
work she had been doing in London. She knew little
more about the new deal going through than she had
known then, other than that it was actually happening.
Before leaving home she had had a dazzling picture of
herself always at Nik's right hand, rapidly becoming
indispensible. Such an image was rapidly fading.

Once, when she protested that she never got to the
company's central offices, he said he needed someone
here. While admitting that this was possible, she
couldn't help feeling something was wrong, and she was
frankly puzzled. There was a lot, she suspected, which
was being deliberately kept from her, and each day she
became increasingly convinced that Nik didn't completely trust her.

This both hurt Vicky and worried her. Why was he so
determined to keep her out of the way? Why had he
brought her here at all if he had so little faith in her?

One evening, after Gordon had left to go to a party
with friends, she found the courage to ask him. She had
spent a busy afternoon and to her surprise Nik invited
her out for a meal. There was no hurry, he said, his
glance sliding comprehensively over the neat blue skirt
and white blouse she was wearing. She could take her
time changing, they needn't leave for another hour.

Vicky's eyes brightened at such a prospect and her foolish heart beat faster, until it suddenly occurred to her that this might be all part of a campaign to keep her in ignorance of what was going on. A candlelit dinner somewhere, to soothe away her growing suspicions? Before she could stop herself, she heard herself exclaiming. 'Sometimes I feel you don't trust me, Mr Demetrious?'

His brows rose arrogantly and she suddenly knew he wasn't accustomed to being challenged like this. Seeing his eyes harden, she expected him to be furious, and felt almost weak with relief when after a second he merely asked quietly, 'Why should you think that?'

She nearly climbed down then and offered an apology. She had a feeling that this was what he was waiting for. If resentment hadn't been burning her up for days she might never have said anything. Licking the tip of her tongue over dry lips, she managed to say defiantly, 'I believe there's a lot going on I don't know about.'

'And you think you should?' His voice was still deceptively gentle.

'Well, shouldn't I?' she muttered rebelliously, trying to bolster a failing determination. 'Most secretaries seem to know everything.'

'Not quite everything, Miss Brown.' His eyes narrowed as he stared at her; this time there could be no mistaking the angry glitter in them. 'When a big take-over is in the last stages of negotiation the least slip can cost a fortune.'

'I hope I've proved I'm discreet!' she whispered stiffly, wishing as she always did when it came to a confrontation with him that she'd had the sense not to begin.

'You haven't proved a thing yet,' his glance pierced her coldly, 'but I shouldn't worry too much, Miss Brown. It's more a matter of caution on my part, rather than an unwillingness to trust you, and I'm sure I give you enough to do.'

Numbly Vicky nodded, wondering why she should still be doubtful. What he said surely made sense. She'd be very silly to believe that every time he didn't tell her something it was an attack on her personal integrity.

'I'm sorry,' she sighed, her blue eyes clouding. 'Now you won't want to take me out to dinner.'

'Don't be so childish,' he snapped impatiently. 'Go and get ready.'

She didn't give him another chance to change his mind but went immediately. After a leisurely bath she slipped on one of the dresses she had bought in London, a silky creation of understated elegance. It was a more stylish dress than she had ever possessed before and she loved the soft, rainbow colours. The low bodice was edged with the same silver threads that were woven into the narrow belt which clasped her slim waist, while the slightly bouffant skirt swirled enticingly about her long, slender legs. The only thing she felt rather dubious about was the neckline, which did seem to leave a lot of her skin bare. She hoped Nik wouldn't think it too daring. After all, he had only asked her out for dinner, not a gala evening.

It was too late to change again now, she decided, having already done her face and hair. Her hair looked nice since she had had it cut. It wasn't so straight any more but tended to riot in tumbled curls around her small, regal head. Gazing at herself in the mirror, before she went out, she tried to squash another twinge of doubt. She didn't look at all like her usual self, but she persuaded herself that Nik might never notice.

He was waiting for her in the lounge wearing a dark dinner jacket, expertly tailored to fit his broad shoulders like a glove. His hard, handsome face was quite expressionless as when she opened the door he turned to watch her approach. The sight of him almost took her breath away, but she could see she didn't have the same effect.

His heavy lids came half down, but his eyes remained

cool as he said briefly, 'Hello, Vicky, you're looking very smart.'

She hadn't expected to be met with open arms, as he might have had time to consider how she had provoked him earlier, but she couldn't help wondering why he spoke so grimly. The words he uttered sounded more-like an insult than a compliment, and she shivered, knowing she would have given anything to have heard him say she looked lovely. He had called her Vicky, though, which he had only done once before, and it proved a balm to her aching disappointment.

Uncertainly she smiled at him, determined to ignore a contempt which perhaps didn't really exist. 'I'm sorry if I'm late, Mr Demetrious.'

'No, you're not,' he replied brusquely, taking the light wrap from her arm, as she paused beside him, and draping it around her shoulders. 'And you'd better call me Nik.'

As his hands touched her something shot through her and she shivered. Feeling it, he turned her swiftly to him. 'Are you cold?' he asked, frowning.

Nervously she shook her head, trying to move away from him. The tightening grip of his hands started fires burning in her body which she didn't know how to control. She had never felt anything like it before and she wasn't sure whether the flames that swept through her were making her sick or giddy. For a moment longer Nik held her, staring into her dazed eyes. 'Then why are you trembling?'

'I don't know,' she replied, quite truthfully.

His eyes flickered. 'Was it because I asked you to call me Nik, or because I touched you?'

Her face coloured hotly and she stiffened. 'Does it have to be anything? I could be trembling with fear and nervousness.'

'Is one so very different from the other?' He smiled suddenly, doing more damage to her already vulnerable heart. 'No, don't answer that. If I ask any more questions you'll soon be fainting from hunger and whatever you're suffering from will only get worse. What I want to know will keep, at least for a few more days.'

How could she resist him, Vicky wondered despairingly, when he smiled at her like that? She supposed it was known as turning on the charm, and Nik Demetrious had more than his fair share of it. He was clever enough too, she suspected, to know exactly how to use it. Hadn't she seen him using it before on other women? She wished she could forget the one on the plane. Yet it was sheer heaven to have him smiling at her instead of growling for a change. And, although Vicky despised herself for her weakness, she found herself responding to him just as helplessly as everyone else did.

Since leaving the apartment he appeared to have changed. He didn't let her out of his sight and he was so attentive she felt she must be dreaming. While it might not be that far removed from reality, she had to admit it was different from the nightmare of frayed nerves she usually experienced whenever she was so near a man. When Nik first asked her to dance she waited for the familiar feeling of repulsion to present itself, but she had felt only the slightest twinge, then it had gone. As his arms tightened round her slender body, she did feel a quiver of something, but it wasn't that.

Glancing up at him, she found his dark gaze fixed on her. Flushing a little, she defensively lowered her head again and closed her eyes. The nightclub where he had brought her for dinner had taken most of her breath away without having him personally removing the last of it. There seemed every likelihood of that happening if he continued staring at her as he was doing and holding her so closely.

Attempting to divert herself a little, Vicky glanced at the other couples around them. She had never seen so many beautiful women and well dressed man before. If

some of the women weren't actually beautiful, the
clothes they wore and their sophisticated hair-styles and
make-up made them so. Nik had pointed out one or
two celebrities, but otherwise he had shown no interest.

Vicky was still feeling dazed by the splendour of this
superb place on the Rockefeller Plaza, and she
wondered humbly what she had done to deserve such
an outing. She refused to spoil an evening which she
was sure she would remember for the rest of her life by
imagining Nik had brought her here to soothe his
conscience, but she wished she could think of another
reason. He was no stranger to New York. There must
be many women, much more attractive than herself,
whom he could have taken out if he had wished, and
she wasn't at all sure that he had a conscience, or, if he
had, that he would let it trouble him.

They had dinner with a view over the city, sixty-five
floors up. As soon as they arrived Nik Demetrious was
immediately recognised, and Vicky noted the red-carpet
treatment he received. They were given one of the best
tables and conducted there like royalty. Feeling more
like a princess every minute, Vicky had difficulty in
suppressing a schoolgirlish giggle as she wondered what
the snooty head waiter would think if he knew she was
merely a common secretary.

Nik had glanced at her after the first five minutes.
'Enjoying yourself?'

'Oh, yes.'

'You approve of such places?' He had sounded
suddenly very foreign.

Eagerly she had nodded, not pretending to be less
than dazzled. 'I still like picnics and meals on a tray,
but this is nice for a change.'

She had meant it as a joke, but it didn't seem to
amuse him. 'You wouldn't be so relaxed if you weren't
used to such places?' he had persisted.

She had glanced at him guiltily, conscious of a note
of censure in his voice. Why should it annoy him that

such opulent surroundings didn't make her tremble
nervously? Occasionally her father had taken her out
and once he had had plenty of friends. He had known a
lot of people, mostly academics, who had been forever
out and in the house—that was until he had remarried.
She wondered how many of them ever thought of her
now.

Immersed in her thoughts, Vicky suddenly realised
she hadn't answered Nik's question, and she was afraid
of how he might have interpreted her silence when his
eyes darkened on her abstracted face.

'Never mind,' he had said curtly, before she had been
able to pull herself together and explain, 'I can guess.'

What about? Wishing he wasn't such an enigma, she
had gazed at him anxiously. Meeting his eyes was like
being exposed to lightning, bright and searing and very
cold! 'Mr Demetrious . . .' she began.

'Nik!' he cut in abruptly. Then, with a shrug which
expressed nothing clearly, he rose to his feet. 'Come on,'
he had said coolly, 'let's dance.'

Willingly she had gone into his arms. She would tell
him about her father when she knew him better. She
was sure this wasn't the time.

Much later she smiled up at him as they danced
again. 'The Rainbow Room,' she murmured dreamily,
'I must have known.'

'I noticed the colour of your dress,' he teased, quite
able, with his quick intelligence, to guess instantly what
she was talking about. 'I've been studying it,' he
informed her solemnly, quite impervious when she
dared cast him a glance of mocking disbelief. 'It's
charming and the colours are so subtle it's difficult to
pick out an individual shade. I'm still trying to decide
whether the green is really blue, or the other way
round.'

Vicky laughed, quite eager to bask in his restored
good humour, especially when it contained no cruelty.
And she knew instinctively that he would be quite

capable of being extremely cruel to a woman, if she displeased him. There was a hardness about him, a strength of purpose which boded ill for anyone he considered had transgressed. She found herself hoping fervently she never would.

He wasn't displeased with her now, though. Vicky could see that, not so much from his eyes, which were often unreadable even when he was in a good mood, but from the predatory, slightly satisfied smile that curved his strong mouth. If something about his smile faintly disturbed her, she grew too bemused, as the evening wore on, to try and discover what it was. They were both good dancers. She had always been light on her feet and their steps matched beautifully. A harmonious silence fell between them as they moved closely together, each deriving such great pleasure from finding the perfect partner as to make words unnecessary. If Vicky's legs trembled occasionally, causing her to stumble, Nik didn't appear to notice. If he did he merely used it as an excuse to hold her even closer.

On her part, Vicky fought desperately against an urge to cling. Nik's vibrant voice and virile body had aroused a response that had quickened her pulses to an alarming degree. She knew an aching need to be closer to him in every way, and she wondered despairingly if she could have fallen in love with him.

It was well after midnight before they returned to the apartment. 'I feel like Cinderella,' Vicky laughed as she paused outside her bedroom door to wish Nik goodnight.

'Would I do as a prince?' he grinned down at her from his great height, watching the colour run enchantingly under her fine skin. 'All I require, isn't it, is a glass slipper?'

'That was a silly thing to say,' she stammered, wondering what on earth he could be thinking.

His mouth quirked lazily. 'In New York I guess one

says and does things one wouldn't elsewhere. It might even be permissible for a man to kiss his secretary goodnight.'

Her startled eyes widened with instant fright as she realised the sudden purpose in his. 'I'm sure it wouldn't be, Nik. I have to remember who I am.'

'You aren't anything tonight but a beautiful woman,' he said coolly, as she edged nearer her bedroom door.

Her retreat was cut off by the iron circle of his arm enclosing her waist, and her gasping protest was just so much wasted breath.

When she tried to escape him, his hand came up her spine to allow his fingers to tangle in her pale, cornsilk hair which he grasped by its tender roots and tugged until it forced her head back. Helplessly she tried to push him away, but her hands were trapped against the hardness of his muscular chest while the lower half of her was crushed between him and the door.

Vicky couldn't avoid his descending mouth or the steel band of his embrace. She hadn't even time to whip up any resistance as he kissed her gently, then with a hard, relentless insistence that sent the blood racing through her veins so fast she thought her body might never contain it.

As the pressure of his mouth suddenly increased, her head was filled with a kind of wild music. It seemed evocative and wildly exciting, arousing her unbearably. Under his ruthless lips her own softened helplessly as he drank so deeply of their sweetness she came near to fainting. All evening she had secretly dreamt of such a moment, but now it had come she couldn't cope with it. She felt shaken out of her whole existence as Nik continued kissing her and his hands moved searchingly over her, not stopping until they curved over the tumultuous rise and fall of her breasts.

The next instant she was released and trying to gather her scattered wits into some semblance of order. A pair of grey eyes glittered over the vivid flush in her cheeks.

A hint of derision still lingered as he said slowly, 'Are you trying to pretend you haven't been kissed before?'

It was so near the mark that the heat in her cheeks increased, but she was saved from answering by Gordon's arrival. He must have been right behind them, and while she felt a flicker of relief from knowing that he hadn't caught her in Nik's arms, she didn't feel so happy about the sudden glint of curiosity in his eyes. Murmuring a hasty goodnight to them both, she retreated into her bedroom.

The next morning she woke with a headache and looked almost resentfully at Nik when she caught him polishing off a large breakfast.

'Good morning, Vicky.' Tall and handsome, he rose to his feet, his eyes intently studying her pale face. 'How are you? You don't look so good.'

'I'm fine, thanks,' she lied, sitting down because even to see him made her feel weak. 'I'm sorry I slept in,' it wasn't yet eight o'clock. 'Is there something you'd like me to do, other than what you've already left for me?'

'No,' he flicked a quick glance at his watch, 'that should keep you busy for the next few hours. I want you to be ready to come out with me, though, after lunch.'

'A business meeting?'

She was startled to discover this wasn't the case, as he smiled and shook his head. 'I'd like to take you on a tour of the city,' he explained. 'You can't go home without seeing something of it.'

Vicky swallowed, unable to hide her surprise. It was so seldom he smiled at her so early in the morning, and on top of this his invitation was completely unexpected.

'Will you come, Vicky?' he asked before she had time to accept, his tone of voice unbelievably urgent.

'I'd love to!' She returned his smile dazedly, her eyes like twin stars, uncaring that Gordon was standing in the doorway and must have heard at least some of their conversation, or that he was betraying even more concern than he had shown the night before.

Would Nik remember? She worried all morning, conscious that if he didn't the disappointment might kill her. Her headache cleared up, then returned again as she found it impossible to relax. She made several mistakes, and it didn't help to realise both the mistakes and headache were due to the same thing.

She was so tense with anxiety she couldn't eat more than a sandwich for lunch, after which she hopefully changed. When Obelia came to tell her that Nik was back and waiting, she didn't try and hide her relief.

With a radiant face she snatched up her bag and went to join him, and some expression in his eyes, as they slipped over her, made her heart miss a beat. She was aware that she looked very nice in her new cotton sundress, but she warned herself not to take him too seriously. He might be, for once, putting himself out on her behalf, but on his part it might just be a whim. He was, after all, her boss, and he probably considered he was entitled to indulge himself now and again. And although Vicky feared her feelings might be involved more than she cared to admit, she wasn't such a fool as to think he would ever reciprocate them. A Greek tycoon wasn't for her and she'd do well to remember it!

Nevertheless she couldn't stop her insides dissolving as her eyes travelled as curiously as his own. He was wearing a pair of casual, jean-type pants and an open-necked shirt, such as she had never seen on him before, and his lean body seemed to take on new and rugged dimensions. Now she could believe in the ancestral peasants he had mentioned, men whose very strength had torn a healthy living from a reluctant soil and whose descendants went on to build empires. A glimpse of a broad, hair-roughened chest, which a half-buttoned shirt left disturbingly bare, drove the breath from her lungs, and she averted her eyes quickly.

He was still staring at her lovely, delicate face. It was

unavoidable that he noticed her agitation. Almost curtly he said, 'You look the picture of threatened innocence, Vicky. I wonder how you manage it?'

Soft furious colour swept into her cheeks. Why should any suggestion of innocence about her seem to annoy him? She almost retorted, 'Because I am,' but how could a girl make such a confession, in this day and age? It would be too naïve to sound convincing.

'You'll be telling me next that you are!' she was startled to hear him gibe.

'Perhaps I am.' His taunt forced the admission she had vowed not to make past stiff lips before she realised.

Nik rarely smiled, but now one did curve his strongly cut mouth, and she was trying nervously to decide what kind of a smile it was when his chauffeur appeared.

'Where are we going?' she asked as the car began edging through the traffic and across Fifth Avenue. On either side of them skyscrapers soared to unbelieveable heights, and while she never ceased to be impressed and thrilled by such evidence of monumental engineering, she was secretly a little afraid of them and sometimes wondered what would happen if they toppled down.

Nik Demetrious lay back against the luxurious upholstery, arms folded, watching her glancing at the skyscrapers apprehensively. 'I told you—a tour. You can take your choice. We can do it by boat or helicopter, or even walk.'

'I'd better leave it to you,' she said, after a moment's hesitation. 'I've no idea which way is best.'

'I suggest we stay with the car,' he replied lightly. 'We might finish up by doing a little walking in Central Park and reserve the helicopter for tomorrow.'

Vicky didn't dare believe that the last half of his sentence was anything more than an idle remark, but she nodded happily. 'I suppose you've seen it all before?' Some of her pleasure faded as she thought he looked rather bored.

Suddenly, to her relief, he smiled again, his broad shoulders lifting briefly. 'I have done, but so long ago that I've probably forgotten what most of it looks like. New York is a working city, and the work and pressure doesn't leave one much time for looking at the view.'

Her smooth brow creased. 'You come here a lot, though.'

His eyes touched her sideways, correctly assessing her frowning face. 'Do you disapprove of my being here or of the way I work?'

'I'm not sure,' she confessed honestly, astonished by her own temerity. 'Perhaps a bit of both? You do work too hard and occasionally you look tired. It might be better if you had a place out of town where you could relax.'

'Nicer for my staff too?' his mouth quirked cynically. 'A country estate with all the right amenities?'

Why must he always be so suspicious of people's motives? 'I can't speak for the others,' she replied sharply, 'but I wasn't even thinking of myself.'

'I'm sorry.' He didn't look it as he continued silkily, 'I'm sure you have my welfare at heart, Miss Brown, but you forget one thing. My homeland is Greece, and if I spend less time there than anywhere else, that is where my heart is.'

What did he know of the heart he talked of so glibly? Vicky, in angry frustration, turned her head from him quickly to stare blindly through the car window. He was a man motivated by strong emotions, she had sensed this when he had kissed her the previous evening, but how often was his heart affected? How much real tenderness had he ever given to any place or woman? He had affairs, but she doubted if his feelings were ever involved to any great extent. At his age it didn't seem fair that he had escaped so lightly while a girl like herself, who did her best to avoid any amatory contact with the opposite sex at all, should feel irrevocably committed to a man who would never love her.

Her eyes misty with tears, she wished he had never kissed her. Part of her was still shocked by the overwhelming physical response he had generated. She had spent the rest of the night trying to dissect the feelings he had aroused in her. She remained bewildered that he had so easily melted inhibitions she had thought too ingrained to be any way removable, yet, glancing at him now, she was even more bewildered by the longing she knew to be in his arms again. It didn't make sense after the years she had spent keeping men at a distance, and she sighed deeply.

Believing her sigh to be caused by discomfort, Nik immediately asked if she was too hot. 'August isn't the best time to come here. It's too humid.'

'I don't really mind it,' she said, letting him think it was, adding in a shaking voice that had his eyes narrowing curiously, 'It will probably be raining when we return to England.'

Vicky found touring Manhattan by car exciting but very confusing—there was so much to take in. They began at the southernmost tip of the island. Nik showed her Wall Street first, one of the oldest parts. It was here, he said, that in 1653 Dutch settlers had built their wall of tree trunks to protect themselves from raiding Indians. It was now the financial district of an area which also contained the twin towers of the World Trade Centre, higher than the Empire State Building by about eight storeys. Other sights he pointed out included the New York Stock Exchange and the Federal Reserve Bank.

Noting wryly how familiar Nik was with the district, Vicky wondered how much business he did there. After an hour they went on through the Lower East Side and Chinatown, names she didn't recognise as she did Greenwich Village. This area was supposed to be rather Bohemian, but she didn't see anything to confirm this reputation. The streets appeared perfectly normal, with nothing more decadent than a few young mothers pushing prams and old gentlemen exchanging gossip.

It didn't look much like a village either, and Nik laughed when she mentioned this and asked what had she expected. Harlem, he said, might surprise her too. True, it did contain many crumbling tenement blocks, but there were plenty of attractive lanes as well as Columbia University.

He decided, however, as the day wore on, to give Harlem a miss, that they would spend what was left of the afternoon in Central Park, over eight hundred acres of landscaped open ground in the centre of the city. He instructed his chauffeur where to drop them and when to pick them up. After which, he informed a slightly dazed Vicky, they would go on somewhere out of town for dinner. And the chauffeur they would leave behind!

Frequently, during the next few days, Vicky felt she must be dreaming, and if it was a dream she hoped she might never wake up. Nik took her everywhere. After touring Manhattan by car, he showed her the city by boat and helicopter, and she loved every minute of it. Many of the famous skyscraper buildings had observation decks, so she not only saw them but went inside them. She came across so many famous names, such as the United Nations headquarters, that she began writing them down, something Nik soon detected and commented on.

'Why?' A dark brow quizzically raised, he took the notebook from her, running his eyes over the closely filled pages.

'Just to show my grandchildren, I suppose,' she laughed, then flushed as she realised what she was saying.

As she had feared, he wasn't slow to point out, 'You'll have to get married first, won't you?'

Embarrassed, Vicky bit her lip. Although she had admitted her love for Nik to herself, she had never got as far as that. Attempting to dismiss the subject casually, she shrugged, 'It was only an idle remark.'

'But interesting.'

'Not particularly,' she reinforced her shrug with a bright smile. 'It's a common enough remark in England. You know the kind of thing. People buy a fabulous piece of jewellery or property, or maybe they just preserve an old photograph or handkerchief, and say it's to show their grandchildren. The same applies . . .'

'Vicky,' he cut in wryly, 'that's universal—you're not telling me something I don't know. I'm not interested in other people's grandchildren, but I might be in yours.'

Didn't he realise how cruel he was being? Her small, flushed face paled. 'I'm not likely to have any.'

'You never know,' he said mildly, taking her hand and turning it over, raising her soft white palm to his lips. As he kissed it twice, she watched, her heart in her eyes. Something urgent stirred in her, struggling for release. This was only the second time he had kissed her and she wanted, shamelessly, to ask him to kiss her properly. A clever girl can always let a man know she is willing, without having to actually put it in words. How many times had she heard girls in the office expressing this view, and she wished unhappily that she had a little more of their experience. How, she wondered, staring desperately down on Nik Demetrious's dark, bent head, did they do it?

CHAPTER FOUR

As he felt her tremble, Nik raised his head and folded her fingers carefully over the place where his firm mouth had been. While her heart tripped crazily, he merely said coldly. 'A small thank you for the pleasure of your company last night.'

Uneasily Vicky tried to control her racing pulses as she watched him picking up his briefcase in readiness to leave the apartment. When he turned with a slight smile, in the dining-room door, to say he would see her later, she was able to nod with a convincing degree of composure.

As the door closed behind him, she remained where she was for a moment, staring apprehensively after him, the hand he had kissed clenched so tightly it began to hurt. Something was wrong; she wished she knew what it was. The artificial smile she had pinned on her lips faded as she tried to define some difference she sensed in Nik's attitude. Could it be her fault? She hadn't really enjoyed herself last night; and perhaps some of the depression she had tried hard to conceal had unconsciously affected him.

Nik had taken her to a cocktail party. He had said he frequently received invitations and liked to accept some of them. When she had demurred that it might not be her thing, he had replied cynically that he thought she might welcome change of company. What he meant by that she had still been trying to puzzle out as they had arrived. She had tried to feel pleased that he was apparently willing to introduce her to his friends, but they weren't the kind of friends she would have chosen for herself. The women had been mostly models and actresses and much too sophisticated for her to believe they could ever have much in common. They were beautiful enough, though, and many were escorted by good-looking men. The apartment had been crowded, thick with smoke and noise and laughter. Vicky had tried hard to pretend she was enjoying herself, but failed. She couldn't be surprised that Nik had eventually deserted her for more cheerful—and glamorous—company. She didn't want to think of the lovely redhead who had wound her slender arms around his neck and kissed him so expertly on the lips.

A black mood can take a lot of getting rid of, and Vicky might have remained depressed if Nik hadn't rung later in the afternoon to ask how she was and to remind her of their date that evening.

'I'm finding it very hard to concentrate,' he growled. 'You're a little minx. I hope you know what you're doing.'

None of his statements might have been very explicit, but merely talking to him was enough to make Vicky feel wonderful again.

Since he had warned her that he might be late, she wasn't surprised that Gordon was in before him. He joined her in the lounge and after a quick glance at her glowing face, cleared his throat uneasily.

'Vicky——' he began.

She looked at him quickly. It wasn't often Gordon sounded hesitant. Apart from Nik, he was one of the most decisive men she had ever met. 'What is it?' she smiled with teasing encouragement. 'Are you after a loan?'

His face tinged with red, he started to stammer, which confused her even more. 'Of course not!'

Solemnly she explained, 'It was only a thought.'

Gordon sighed, still hesitating. 'I'm trying to offer you some advice, Vicky, but it's not very easy. Not when Nik's my boss and I respect him. In nearly every way he's a brilliant man . . .'

Vicky's face sobered suddenly. 'I believe you're trying to warn me about something?'

'Yes,' his voice rushed, 'if you'll listen.'

Vicky said in a rush, too, 'Gordon, I am twenty-two!'

'I'm not talking of years. You're only a child in many ways. The difference in years wouldn't matter, but the difference in experience does.'

Vicky frowned, her cheeks colouring hotly. 'So it is Nik and me we're discussing?'

He nodded somewhat miserably.

She tried to be patient, because Gordon meant to be kind. He was cautious; he always looked for the pitfalls in any situation before he gave a thought to the advantages. He mightn't consider the emotions warranted a different approach from a business deal. 'Most men over thirty, I suppose, are experienced to some degree.'

'Damn!' she heard him mutter frustratedly, under his breath.

'Stop alarming yourself, Gordon,' she begged, if a little tautly, as something in his manner began getting under her skin. 'Nik's been good to me, but that's all.' She took a deep breath before she was able to say calmly, 'I never imagine he's going to fall in love with me.'

Gordon said tersely and, she thought, somewhat irrelevantly, 'Nik might be cosmopolitan and he does have other blood in his veins, but he's predominantly Greek. He does have strong prejudices.'

'What has that to do with me?' Vicky cried, almost belligerently, wanting to cover her ears. 'I hope I know my place.'

'It's not that, Vicky,' Gordon pressed on hoarsely. 'What I'm telling you is for your own good. Nik doesn't take women seriously. A man would be blind not to see you're a little thoroughbred, but that's not the point. I'll give Nik his due, he never asks for credentials, but marriage would be something entirely different, and I wouldn't like to see you hurt.'

'There's nothing between Nik and myself,' she assured him.

Gordon continued to look doubtful. 'All the same, he has taken you out a lot.'

'Perhaps it's just a whim.' Vicky voiced her own suspicions of a few days ago.

'Just as long as you realise,' he muttered stiffly.

That evening, Nik was taking her out into the country again for dinner. She had been impressed by the valley of the Hudson River, which they had explored a few days previously. Nik had shown her the Military Academy at West Point and the homes of the Vanderbilts and Franklin D. Roosevelt at Hyde Park. That was over ninety miles away and she didn't think they would be going as far or exploring tonight, but she guessed it would be somewhere they would both like.

She sighed almost ruefully at the thought of going home again, as they would be in a day or two, because she was only just beginning to find her way around. This afternoon, for instance, she had dared snatch a couple of hours off, in Nik's absence, and gone out alone. On Fifth Avenue she had bought a new dress. She had never seen anything like the fabulous stores to be found there and she had told Obelia laughingly, when she'd returned, that it was perhaps just as well she didn't live here permanently, or she might be tempted to spend every penny she had!

She didn't really need a new dress, but she hadn't been able to resist it. As the assistant had packed it, her own extravagance had worried her. Now that she had it on she couldn't help feeling satisfied with the results, and her conscience settled down. Happily she dabbed perfume on her unsteady pulses before adding another whirl of mascara and running out to meet Nik.

If she had had any lingering doubts about her appearance, the sharpening intentness of his gaze would have whipped them away. She heard his breath catch and rasp in his throat as she came upon him in the lounge.

Hearing her approaching, he swung round. For one

sickening moment she thought he looked contemptuous, but it must only have been a trick of the light. When she blinked and glanced at him again he was smiling and there was definitely admiration in his eyes.

'You're looking very lovely this evening, Vicky. A new dress?'

'Yes.' She felt so good she laughed up at him, unaware of the slight provocation in her face. Despite Gordon's warning, happiness bubbled up inside her as she presented to Nik an entirely different girl from the reticent one he was used to. 'Do you like it?'

'Was it necessary?' he countered teasingly.

Her eyes continued to dance at him, her soft lips tilting. 'It was terribly expensive.'

'I'll reimburse you.'

It was somehow like a slap in the face and she shrank back as if it actually had been. 'Oh, no, I can manage,' she exclaimed.

'If you could you wouldn't have mentioned it,' he said, a faint curl to his lips.

Vicky stared at him, sudden tears choking in her throat, dismayed by his changing attitude. Bleakly she transferred her damp-eyed gaze away from him, wondering why he always blew so hot and cold. He must have a poor opinion of women if he imagined they were always after money—or was his opinion merely confined to his secretary, namely one Vicky Brown? A little sigh escaped her as she decided she might be wiser not to go out this evening. A day which began badly often ended the same way.

As if guessing her intentions, Nik didn't give her a chance to change her mind but let the subject drop while he hustled her outside to the waiting car. For all she despised her own weakness, Vicky was glad to leave before Gordon arrived to add his disapproving stare to Nik's. That, she decided despairingly, might be more than she could stand.

Nik did ask abruptly, as they drove off, where

Gordon had got to, and she said she thought he must be in his room as she had been talking to him an hour ago. She wondered what he would say if she told him what about.

She was surprised, with Nik by her side so coldly silent, at the feeling of relief that swept over her as they left the city. She liked New York, but she liked the country surrounding it even better. She loved the out-of-the-way places where a couple could dine and dance in almost complete privacy. In New York their evenings had often been encroached on by some acquaintance of Nik's but there was little chance of that happening here. Deep in the country she had Nik all to herself, and if it was selfish she knew it wouldn't last long. Once back in London, she didn't suppose he would ever ask her out with him again.

He eventually pulled up at a place by the river, a beautiful spot recommended, he told her, by friends. Vicky had never seen anything like the luxurious, rambling hotel with its wonderful background of water and trees. She thought it one of the most romantic places she had seen and found herself relaxing in a way she wouldn't have believed possible an hour earlier. In the peaceful atmosphere of secluded tables and soft-footed waiters, she felt the last of her tension slide from her when Nik began smiling at her again and apologised for his bout of bad temper.

'I'm sorry,' he looked at her ruefully, 'I've had rather a hectic afternoon, then Gordon disappeared.'

'He——' Vicky hesitated, 'he did say everything had been concluded very successfully.'

'Well, yes,' Nik grunted impatiently, 'but there's still enough to do.'

'You're tired?' Noting the unusual paleness of his face, Vicky thought she understood. She wished she had the right to place her hand compassionately over his as it lay on the table. The most she dared was to touch it lightly, hoping this would convey her sympathy.

He stared at her hand as she nervously withdrew it, his mouth tightening. 'Yes,' he admitted, 'but soon I expect to feel a whole lot better.'

'When you get home?' she suggested, then remembered his home wasn't hers. 'Nik?' she murmured uncertainly, her beautiful blue eyes barely meeting his, 'would you say you were prejudiced at all?'

He glanced at her sharply. 'In what way?'

Pretending a casualness she didn't feel, she contrived to answer carelessly, 'Oh, how the Greeks still believe in the vendetta, for instance.'

His eyes darkened angrily. 'Must we discuss this right now, Vicky?'

'Why, no ...' She wished she had never even mentioned it but she hadn't expected such a sharp reaction. 'I have no wish to discuss it, anyway.'

'Then why bring it up?'

As she had expected him to let the subject drop, it confused her when he persisted. 'Does there have to be a reason?' she murmured weakly. 'It was something that just crossed my mind.'

'Really?'

As she stared at the elevated dark brows, they seemed threatening as much as derisive. Vicky shivered, knowing it was impossible that he could have overheard Gordon talking to her but unable to rid herself of a lingering suspicion.

'It's lovely here, isn't it?' She made a desperate, if rather obvious attempt to talk of something else.

Nik, too, appeared willing to make an effort. 'Not as lovely as you are, Vicky.' His eyes rested, with a kind of self-mockery, on her bare shoulders and smooth young neck before wandering over her gleaming head and perfect skin. A mixture of seriousness and amusement lay in their smouldering depth as he added, 'I shall have to make sure I'm not tempted to eat you instead of my dinner!'

The food was so delicious, Vicky doubted it, but relief

at the lighter note in his voice filled her, bringing a smile to her face. After they had finished eating they danced—something, at least, she was sure Nik enjoyed doing with her. As usual their steps matched perfectly and she was strangely content to relax dreamily in his arms. She closed her eyes and sighed deeply as she felt excitement rising too. She loved him, but moments like this were the most she could ever hope for and it was going to take her years and years to get over him. If ever, a small, mocking voice said.

Later they went for a walk beside the river. The night was warm and dark, their path illuminated by only a few stars. Vicky needed the arm Nik laid loosely around her waist to guide her, but she could have done without the sensation it aroused. After being so close to him on the dance-floor she would as soon have walked apart, to allow her disturbed senses time to calm down.

As they rounded a corner, the lights of the hotel disappeared. The Hudson River ran deep and there was only the starlit water to throw shadows from the towering trees lining its banks. Above them a whispering wind moved through the same trees, a lonely but soothing sound. The hotel hadn't been busy and the few other guests apparently preferred to stay there, as there was no one here but themselves. Even so, Nik drew Vicky into the seclusion of some giant oaks until their branches isolated them completely.

He didn't speak, and neither did she, for she suddenly knew he was going to kiss her. Because she wanted it with all her heart, she daren't make a sound for fear he might change his mind. She knew she should be ashamed of such a longing, for allowing it to become like a fever inside her, but she was drawn helplessly by emotions much stronger than the last remains of her common sense. When he stopped and drew her to him, she went into his arms wordlessly, lifting her face to his without a thought of denying the mouth that descended almost savagely.

A lack of tenderness made no difference to her reactions. Heat flamed through her body immediately, as if Nik had just thrown an electric switch. His fingers seemed to burn her skin as he held her chin until his mouth made its first unerring impact. Instinctively her lips parted beneath his devastating invasion and every inch of her body was permeated by a hot, intolerable weakness. Around her his arms tightened, the only thing she was aware of in a world drifting rapidly away. When he raised his head at last, it was merely so he could pick her up and lower her to the soft, still warm grass beneath their feet.

As he came down beside her, he spoke in a low, rough voice. 'You don't mind, Vicky? It's what we both want.'

She wasn't sure of his meaning but was aware of a thrill of near shock. Opening her eyes dazedly, she watched him stripping off his white jacket and loosening his collar.

'Grass stains,' he muttered, as if perfectly conscious of her uncertain gaze. 'Your obvious liking for blue and green won't show.'

She should get up. She was aware of a shiver of fear as she wondered if he meant to seduce her. If he tried she might struggle, but she knew she would be no match for him. He had her head already whirling, her senses swimming. He knew she ached for him, for he must have judged her initial response well enough to feel confident that the next step was going to be easy.

Vicky was still trying to fight her own violent desires as Nik pulled her close again and she heard his soft laughter as the arms she had been holding stiffly by her sides reached out to pull down his head, to bring his sensuous mouth towards the quivering curve of her lips, which were already parting in shameless anticipation.

He kissed her deeply, then ran his lips all over her face while his hands lightly curved her slender body. She made one last attempt to resist, trying to call to her

aid some of the horror of being too close to a man that
had protected her before. When this failed, she gave in
to the weakness which assailed her muscles and the
warm languor creeping through her limbs. Once when
she looked at him through the darkness, she saw a light
blazing fiercely in his eyes until it was screened by his
thick lashes. For a second his expression chilled her,
bringing a return of her senses as none of her own self-
counselling had done, but before she could elude him,
her mouth was imprisoned by his again and she was
kissed bruisingly until all thought of escape finally
vanished.

She strained, fighting the crush of his arms, but their
hardness held her fast as he waited for her resistance to
lessen. Only when it did, did he lift himself a little away
from her in order to slip the narrow straps of her dress
from her bare shoulders, to allow him total access to
the pale smoothness of her full breasts. Deliberately he
trailed his fingertips over the throbbing points before
his mouth moved in to take possession.

An uncontrollable shudder quivered through Vicky
which seemed to reverberate in the long, lean body
lying heavily half over her. As Nik nibbled and played
with her hot skin she was driven to the edge of dizziness
He dominated her, marking his possession as she was
forced to endure the explorations of his plundering
mouth. Her pulses thundered in her ears, a lethal
weakness fast overcoming her as her strength was
drained from her so swiftly she was unable to move.

It was the building up of the emotions pouring
through her so wildly which at last motivated her
sufficiently to wrench herself from his arms. She had
never imagined herself capable of such passion, and she
was frightened it might drive her to doing something
insane. Flushing with humilation, she realised that Nik
was aware of the feelings consuming her as his eyes
glowed mockingly over her shivering, shaking body.

'So,' he muttered thickly, 'for the first time in your

life perhaps, you find something motivating you more powerfully than your mercenary little mind!'

Because the drumming in her ears had not completely subsided, Vicky wasn't sure she had heard properly. 'Nik——' she pleaded unevenly.

'I'm sorry, Vicky. I scarcely know what I'm saying.' It wasn't like Nik not to understand exactly every word he was saying, but in this case his accent was so pronounced she had to believe it. 'My feelings ran away with me,' she heard him continuing. 'I brought you here this evening with the intention of asking you to marry me, not to seduce or insult you, my darling.'

'You're asking me to marry you?' When he nodded she forgot everything else as the wonder of his proposal swept over her, making her face radiant. 'Oh, Nik,' she breathed, 'I do love you!'

He stared at her with a glint of satisfaction in his eyes. 'Does that mean you will?'

'Oh, yes, darling!' She couldn't stop gazing at him. 'I—I did wonder if you wanted an affair. I never for a moment thought you might want to marry me!'

'Why do you think I've been taking you out as much?'

'I thought you were lonely—bored?' she confessed.

He laughed. 'Darling,' he jeered, 'I know plenty of women more than capable of entertaining me if it had only been that.'

Something in his voice worried her again, bringing a troubled shadow to her dazzling blue eyes. 'Nik,' she demurred anxiously, 'you are really certain you want to marry me?'

'Haven't I already said so?'

His voice was curt, but that might be just to stress his point, and marriage was a serious commitment. It was the expression in his eyes as they went insolently over her that bothered Vicky more.

Suddenly she flushed as she realised her state of nakedness and thought she understood his disapproval.

He might have been responsible for the disarray she was in, but that had been before. Now she was his fiancée, he would naturally expect her to behave with more decorum. Hastily, she retrieved her dress from around her waist and pulled the straps back over her shoulders. 'And I've already said yes,' she smiled through misty tears. 'I love you very much.'

She waited for him to declare his own love, but he didn't. He merely laughed and drew her close again, bending his head to take her lips, as if to seal a bargain. This time she strained against him, her arms circling his neck, answering his kisses passionately. Suddenly she felt free and exultant, no longer afraid. 'Darling,' she gasped a few minutes later, burying her hot face breathlessly against him, 'when will we be married?'

He stiffened, she could feel it right through him. 'You are in a hurry?'

He could only be teasing. So why did she notice his tenseness, the harsh note in his voice? She had thought he would want to be married as soon as possible, his lovemaking—her face grew hotter—had given that impression, and she didn't think either of them had anything to wait for. Of course in his country it might not be considered proper to be married almost immediately after the engagement was announced. There wasn't a great deal of difference between the peoples of the world until it came to serious things, such as religion and marriage. But it was almost always the differences of this kind which caused problems.

She sighed, pulling away from him. 'I didn't mean to be presumptuous, Nik—I'm sorry.'

'There are certain formalities,' he replied coolly, without being more explicit. Letting her go, he reached for his jacket. 'I expect we will get round to deciding on a date some time in the future.'

When she wanted only to belong to him! Blindly she glanced upwards, towards the tops of the tall trees, hoping it would be sooner than his tone of voice apeared to indicate. She must buy herself a book on Greek customs. Perhaps he was only following normal procedure in not telling her he loved her and asking her to wait.

'When did you first know you wanted to marry me, Nik?' she asked, as they walked back to the hotel.

'I'm not sure,' he sounded preoccupied. 'Perhaps as soon as I heard about you.'

'Heard about me?'

'Saw you, I mean.'

It was too dark for Vicky to notice his suddenly wary glance. She was content. She had thought he would ask how long she had loved him. From odd things she had read, she had gathered this was the kind of thing couples asked each other, once their love had been declared. But he didn't ask, and she wasn't sure how it would sound if she were to declare starkly that she had loved him almost since she had come to work for him.

It should have been easy to talk to him, now they were engaged, but Vicky was surprised to find how difficult it was. Surely getting engaged couldn't have turned them into strangers? As they left the hotel to drive to New York, she found herself stealing uncertain glances at Nik's powerful profile, wondering what he was thinking of. On this night shouldn't he be thinking only of her? Perhaps, though, it might be as well to hope he wasn't. Suddenly apprehensive, she had a convincing feeling that his thoughts weren't pleasant ones.

What did she actually know of him? she asked herself, while trying not to give her imagination too much rein. He was a very clever man but one, she guessed darkly, with a curious little shiver, capable of violent, even dangerous emotions. Capable of suppressing and disguising them too, she suspected, so that no one might know what he was really thinking.

'Can I tell Gordon and the others about us?' she asked, as they pulled up outside the apartment after what seemed a remarkably silent journey. 'Would you mind?' she pleaded almost timidly.

'For heaven's sake, Vicky!' her humility appeared to annoy him, although he spoke in a low voice. 'Tell them what you like.'

Her lips trembled as he turned on her, and with a muffled exclamation he swept her into his arms. 'Don't mind me,' he muttered thickly against her ear, 'I'm a brute.'

'You're tired.' She clung to this like a sailor to a lifebelt. She didn't really mind what Nik was when he held her like this. He could stop her mind with his hands sliding over her, his kisses, full of urgent desire, on her lips. Her eyes were tremulous and shy when he released her, wholly forgiving.

'I have your engagement ring,' his voice was almost coaxing, as if he was determined to make up for his ill humour. Lightly he laughed. 'The jeweller promised he would take it back if you turned me down. I'll get it as soon as we get in and we can all celebrate.'

'That will be lovely.' Vicky ignore a flicker of disappointment, for she would have liked to have gone with him to choose the ring. When people got engaged wasn't that what they were supposed to do? This must be the way it was done in Greece and, of course, sometimes in England. Didn't men often have the ring secretly hidden away in a pocket?

The sound of music coming from the lounge indicated that Gordon was in and hadn't yet gone to bed. Nik drew Vicky swiftly past the lounge door to his bedroom. Leaving her near the door, he went to open a safe in the wall and returned with a box in his hand.

'There you are,' he smiled, giving it to her.

Rather nervously she took it, fumbling with the catch until the lid flew back, revealing a ring. Uncertainly she stared at it, not quite knowing what she had expected. For one awful moment she had feared Nik might have bought something gaudy and ostentatious, and she was delighted with what she saw. It was a beautiful ring, at least she thought so. It might not have been terribly expensive, although she had no clear idea of the value of such things, but she loved the single blue stone set in a circle of white ones. She realised he must have chosen carefully as the dark blue stone exactly matched her eyes and was so overwhelmed by a wave of love and gratitude she couldn't speak.

'Aren't you going to put it on?' he asked smoothly.

'Oh, yes.' She had been waiting for Nik to do this and she flushed guiltily. Hastily she slipped it on the third finger of her left hand, trying not to feel selfconscious. 'It's lovely,' she thanked him fervently. 'Is it a—a family heirloom?'

'Good heavens, no!' Vicky was startled that he seemed almost affronted. It was only for a second though, as he said suavely, 'A girl like you deserves something quite different.'

She wasn't sure of his meaning, but as it seemed a sore point she didn't pursue it. 'I just wondered,' she shrugged.

'Let's go and tell the others and get it over with.' He pushed her from the room impatiently, his hands hard but no more so than his voice.

Feeling hurt again but deciding she was far too sensitive, Vicky followed him across the hall. 'It's late, darling,' she protested. 'wouldn't in the morning be better?'

Exactly then, Obelia came from the kitchen quarters carrying a tray. 'Oh, hello, sir, miss,' she beamed. 'Philo and I have just come in and I asked Mr Taylor if he would like some coffee. Perhaps you would both like some too?'

'Never mind about coffee, Obelia,' Nik grinned imperiously. 'Go and fetch a bottle of our best champagne. Miss Vicky and I have just got engaged.'

Because he had already flung open the lounge door, Gordon heard and jumped to his feet. Vicky saw his face go a dull red and guessed he was remembering the advice he had made her listen to earlier. She smiled at him warmly, trying to convey silently that she bore him no ill feeling.

Nik moved from behind her, standing apart, watching Gordon through slightly narrowed eyes. 'Did you hear? We're engaged.'

Vicky bit her lip. Why hadn't he put his arm round her and said, Vicky has promised to marry me—Or, I'd like you to meet my future wife? He might simply have completed another business deal, although on such occasions she had known him to show more enthusiasm. She didn't think Gordon had noticed, but it might occur to him later, when things often did.

Obelia hurried back. 'Philo's bringing the champagne,' she cried, very excited. 'I left him to bring it, because I couldn't wait to see your ring, Miss Vicky.'

Proudly Vicky showed it to her, and Obelia's brown eyes examined it eagerly. 'It's very nice,' she said, after a moment's hesitation.

Gordon broke the rather awkward silence, offering his congratulations. 'When I can get a word in!' he grinned, at which Obelia burst into a thousand apologies. 'Oh, what must you think of me!' she exclaimed.

Vicky felt vaguely unreal during the next two days, before they went home again. She told herself she should be one of the happiest girls alive. She would be, she knew, if she could really believe what was happening to her. It couldn't be Nik's fault that she sometimes had doubts, for he was extremely attentive, and with every passing hour she felt she was falling more deeply in love with him. If only she could get rid of the niggling feeling that something was wrong, all would be well. It could only be that Nik was far above her socially. He ought to have been marrying a society girl who would make him a perfect wife. She had to keep in mind that the choice had been his, that he must have had plenty of opportunity to marry someone like this if he'd wanted to. Once Vicky managed to convince herself of this, she felt much better, and as they flew home she was able to relax and even enjoy the journey.

Despite this, her underlying doubts still prevented her from telling him about Vera. He knew her parents were dead and she had no brothers or sisters. Surprisingly he didn't appear to be interested in her family, or what she had done before she met him. Because of his lack of interest, Vicky managed to persuade herself that as Vera had merely been her stepmother there was no real need to mention her at all. If she told him about her stepmother, he might demand to meet her and with his shrewdness might guess immediately what kind of a woman she was. He might naturally think that Vera must have had some influence on her and that she might be the same. Vicky decided apprehensively that she couldn't risk it.

Gordon's reaction to their engagement wasn't altogether clear, although he had congratulated them warmly enough. When he got her alone, the following morning, when Nik was on the phone after breakfast, he had apologised for the advice he had given.

'I feel an awful fool, Vicky,' he'd said ruefully. 'Why didn't you shut me up instead of letting me ramble on like an idiot?'

Vicky bore him no animosity. She could even admire the way he faced up to what could have been an embarrassing situation. Many men might simply have ignored it. 'I'm sure you acted with the best of intentions,' she smiled gently. 'You know I usually value your advice, Gordon.'

'But not in this case.' He had returned her smile wryly, then hesitated, his eyes faintly anxious. 'You know I wish you well, Vicky, and Nik couldn't have found a nicer girl, but, at the risk of seeming a wet blanket, the course of true love doesn't always run smoothly, and if you ever need a shoulder to cry on . . .'

'What a thing to say to a newly engaged girl!' she had teased, while her eyes misted, for she realised Gordon's offer was a genuine one and not lightly given.

On their last day in New York Vicky scarcely saw Nik, but as there was a lot to wind up she didn't expect to. She worked as usual in the apartment, feeling so happy that she forgave Obelia popping in every five minutes on the pretext of seeing if she wanted something but really to talk. That Obelia was excited over the engagement was obvious.

'The next time you come to New York you might be married,' she beamed.

'Perhaps.' Vicky didn't say their marriage was something Nik had avoided discussing.

'Will the wedding be soon?' Obelia enquired happily. 'Philo and I would love to attend, but it will be in Athens or Corfu, will it not?'

'I'm not sure.'

Obelia went on. 'Mr Nik has a wonderful villa on Corfu. I expect that is where you will live and bring up your family.'

Vicky typed a wrong letter and had to correct it. This was something else Nik hadn't mentioned. He had told her about his villa, of course, but not its exact location. She tried to believe there hadn't been time, but she couldn't help wondering why he hadn't taken the opportunity, on their way home the other night, to talk about such things. Nor could she understand why she should find the discovery that his villa was on Corfu so disturbing. She had found Corfu a delightful island and she was sure it would be wonderful to live there.

It was no use making herself miserable, Vicky sighed, swallowing a sudden lump in her throat as Obelia left her. Fiercely she reminded herself that Nik was no ordinary man, and apart from light affairs, was probably used to concentrating mainly on business. If she was going to worry because he appeared to ignore the usual things engaged couples talked about, then perhaps she should begin looking for someone else.

CHAPTER FIVE

IN the offices in London, their engagement proved something more than just a nine days' wonder. While the staff, generally, hid their initial reaction well, Vicky would have had to be very insensitive indeed not to have noticed that the stir it caused amounted in some quarters to near-consternation. There were women more beautiful than herself, who had known Nik Demetrious much much longer and couldn't understand how she had succeeded where they had failed. No one was being stupid enough to risk offending Nik by criticising his future wife openly, but Vicky sensed there was a lot of whispering going on behind her back. She actually overheard one of the secretaries saying to another that there was many a slip twixt the cup and the lip and that little Miss Brown hadn't got Nik Demetrious to the altar yet!

Despite this, during the days which followed their return, Nik took Vicky out almost every night and was so attentive that all her doubts faded. She was able to ignore any spiteful innuendoes and was rapturously happy. Nearly every evening Nik and she dined together, either in his apartment or in some fashionable nightclub, where they could also dance. There had been no engagement party, but he had assured her this wasn't necessary, that he would rather have her to himself in the evenings and there would be plenty of time for socialising later on. He showered her with compliments and small presents, and each morning, before she left for work, a boy arrived from a famous florists with a bouquet of beautiful flowers in which Vicky would bury her radiant, dreaming face.

After three weeks, during which his attention never

wavered, she felt confident enough to ask again about the date of their marriage. It was the first time Nik had agreed to come in for coffee after bringing her home, and this, in itself, seemed to Vicky a good sign. Every other time she had asked him in he had refused. That he didn't appear to like the house worried her a lot. It wasn't that she had any desire to go on living there after they were married, but she had no clear idea what she was going to do with it. She kept wondering how long she would have to get rid of it, and because she felt it was growing imperative that she should know, she plucked up enough courage to ask tentatively if he had given any more thought to a date for their marriage.

They were sitting together on the wide settee in the drawing-room, an elegant room, around which Nik had stared grimly when she had first shown him to it. It was much as it had always been, apart from a few cigarette burns and wine stains left by Vera's friends. She wondered if it was these that bothered him. The night was warm, and after dining out, Vicky felt too happy and replete to do more than wonder. She didn't really need the coffee she had made in the spacious, much too big for one kitchen, but Nik appeared to be enjoying it.

He answered her question lazily, pushing aside his cup to take her lazily in his arms. 'There's plenty of time,' he murmured against her cheek. 'You know how busy I've been. I'm just beginning to relax after New York, but eventually I'll get round to it.'

When he held her, as he was doing, she found it difficult to think seriously. With a resigned little sigh she nodded. 'I love you, Nik,' she murmured indistinctly, as he nibbled the smooth, bare skin of her neck. The warmth of their bodies pressing against each other was already making her languorous and her arms crept round his neck, holding him tightly.

'We'll talk about it one of these days,' he promised softly, undoing the buttons of his shirt and dealing in a similar fashion with those down the front of her dress before pulling her closer. 'But marriage is a serious business—where to live, children, entertaining. I just want to have you to myself a little longer.'

Vicky wanted to argue that marriage could only bring them closer in every way, even closer than they were now. It was difficult to understand, when she had been so apprehensive of men, that she wanted to give herself so completely to Nik, but she did. And if she felt this way then how could Nik, who she suspected was highly sexed, be content to wait? It wasn't as if they were already living together. That was something he had never suggested.

Watching him through lowered lashes, aching for him intensely, she saw the hard lines of his face darken with passion as he caressed her gently. He began kissing her deeply, and everywhere his fingers touched became intolerably sensitive. His hands slid up her spine, exploring it thoroughly, as though he must know every inch of her intimately. His mouth brushed hers lightly as he laid her back on the soft cushions and came down on top of her. He was trembling and she heard his breath rasp even as her own breathing quickened and her heart beat faster.

They hadn't been like this since the night he had asked her to marry him, and they kissed as though they had been parted for years and known nothing in between. She felt the sensuous roughness of his deep chest crushing her breasts and the heaviness of his limbs pressing against her own. His eyes were hollow pits of naked desire as his hands caressed her suddenly taut nipples and she came swiftly alive under his touch. Feeling his mouth fire with passion, Vicky heard herself gasping as he groaned. Nothing much seemed to matter as his kisses grew deeper, more insistent, until they were both moving against each other mindlessly.

'Sleep with me, Vicky,' he demanded huskily. 'Don't deny me tonight.'

It was the last thing she could do. She knew she was

ready to give him anything. And it couldn't be wrong, could it, not when they were engaged. She might be inexperienced, but Nik would know that and make allowances.

'Vicky?'

At the urgent note in his voice she felt a small shiver of fear, but her desire for him was stronger, sweeping away the last of her hesitation. 'Yes,' she whispered, trying to clear her head sufficiently to add breathlessly, 'You do realise if we—if we do, we might have to get married sooner than you'd anticipated?'

Why she said this, Vicky wasn't sure. It must have been that subconsciously she had wanted to remind him of her inexperience, so that if anything happened he wouldn't feel trapped. His continuing reluctance to fix a definite date for their marriage could have instinctively forced such a warning past her trembling lips. She didn't know, either, whether to be glad or sorry when after a few tense moments Nik pulled himself savagely away from her.

'It might not be such a good idea after all,' he muttered harshly, his glittering eyes hooded.

Vicky felt so coldly bereft she didn't think she would ever feel warm again. 'Nik,' she cried raggedly, 'have I said the wrong thing?'

As he shook his head, a wild flush rose to her cheeks. Sitting up, she began refastening the buttons of her dress with fumbling fingers, while Nik looked as though he might resort to something violent. The blaze in his dark eyes suggested it might be folly to argue with him, but she was still disturbed enough to be able to ignore the advice of her instincts.

'If we're going to be married,' she pleaded, with a lack of shame that mortified her when she thought of it later, 'can it really matter what we do?'

Again he hesitated tensely. 'A Greek doesn't marry a woman he has slept with.'

She was beginning to see, but at the same time she

couldn't help feeling stunned by his apparent ability to turn his emotions on and off so easily. If he had any real emotions! Had he ever said he loved her? Bewildered, she stared at him, her blue eyes stormy, her rumpled hair falling carelessly over her thin young shoulders. Tears of frustration scalded her eyes as he gazed back at her implacably. It was a quality she immediately recognised in him. He had made up his mind and nothing would change it.

'I'll go now, Vicky.' The coldness of his voice warned her not to make a scene while she felt like screaming.

Hating him, loving him, she scrambled to her feet, trying to contrive a little dignity. 'I'll show you out,' she muttered incoherently, hurrying past him. At the door she sought for something normal to say so he wouldn't notice her agitation. 'This house is too big for me. I'm going to sell it.'

He stiffened, eyes narrowed as he paused under the columned portico outside. 'When?'

'If we're going to be married, soon,' she replied, wishing she had never said anything. The house never pleased him—she had been a fool to mention it.

He made no comment as he bent to kiss her, the touch of his mouth so brief she wondered why he bothered.

'Goodnight,' she breathed, close to tears. 'I love you, Nik.'

Her voice followed him, a mere whisper, but he might have heard it as he glanced at her cynically over his shoulder as he got into his car.

When he had gone, Vicky flew back to bury her now tear-wet face in the cushions of the settee where they had been sitting. As soon as he left she realised how tired she was, but there was an urgent need inside her to recapture some of the moments she and Nik had shared here. The cushions they had lain on were still warm, but in the morning would be as cold as his eyes had been when he walked away from her. As cold as his love!

Why should she think that? It was foolish to imagine he didn't love her, why else would he be marrying her? She had neither wealth nor outstanding good looks. Questions without answers raced wildly through Vicky's head until she felt dizzy. Pushing distracted fingers through her still tumbled hair, she sat up and rested her elbows on her knees, her face in her hands. She didn't feel ashamed of having offered herself to Nik. She had promised to marry him, which must mean she had more or less given herself to him already. It was always a source of wonder to her that his kisses thrilled instead of frightening her. That she could think of belonging to him completely with scarcely a qualm seemed an even greater miracle.

The one thing she longed for now, above everything, was to hear Nik saying he loved her, and she couldn't understand her growing certainty that this might never happen. She had known something was happening to her long before she realised what it was, but Nik might never have experienced the same vibrations. She didn't believe he would deny the strange magnetism which drew them together, but this on its own could be merely physical attraction. And if he was just attracted to her physically, Vicky wondered despairingly what sort of basis that would make for marriage, and how long it would be before he tired of her.

She spent an almost sleepless night, suddenly sure that he was tired of her already, and was reluctant to see him again to hear him tell her so. When she did arrive at the office he was exactly the same as usual and she was overwhelmed by a crazy kind of relief. He discussed only business and was in such a good mood that her relief contrarily gave way eventually to bitterness, that what had occurred the previous evening had left him so obviously undisturbed.

As they lunched together his good mood continued, and although he still kept off personal matters, he did tell her she looked lovely and that he liked the dress she was wearing. He ordered champagne and after her second glass Vicky was ready to forgive him anything, even if he didn't ask.

That evening he had a dinner engagement with an old friend, he said. Vicky, concluding that it was someone he didn't want her to meet, was pleased enough to have an evening to herself for a change. There were a lot of chores to catch up on and she might, if she had time, pop in and see Mrs Younger. She hadn't seen much of her since returning from New York and she didn't want her to feel neglected and hurt.

The next day was a busy one at the office, with calls coming in from all over the world. Nik was closeted with Gordon for the greater part of it, and he kept her running continually in and out. Vicky was thankful for her growing competence which enabled her to cope with his sometimes unreasonable demands, but occasionally she couldn't help wondering if he had forgotten she was his fiancée.

She realised he hadn't when he told her he was taking her to a party that evening, after they finished. Vicky was delighted, until his following remark brought back all her recent fears.

'It's time we circulated a bit more,' he said crisply, 'otherwise we might grow tired of each other.'

All the time she dressed Vicky tried not to ask herself what he meant. He hadn't bothered to explain, and before she could make up her mind to challenge him about it, the telephone rang and he had waved her out of the office. Gordon was waiting to take her home, he had said, and he would pick her up later.

Now she decided that he had had a trying day and hadn't really intended upsetting her. If nothing else happened she might be wiser to let the matter drop.

Refusing to think of the times she had advised herself to do this, Vicky dressed with extra care. Knowing she looked good helped her composure, as did the quick flicker of admiration in Nik's eyes when he came, as he had promised, to collect her. She basked in his apparent approval without realising how she was coming to covet every kind word and glance he spared her, like a starving man might pounce on a few crumbs.

As though to make up for his ill humour throughout the day, Nik kissed her lightly and helped her tenderly into the car, so that she soon felt happy again. As they drove out of London she asked who was giving the party, and he gave the name of a well known personality and his wife. 'Friends of mine,' he said.

Vicky knew the man he mentioned had a title, but she didn't say anything. She had worked for Nik for several weeks and was aware he had a wide circle of acquaintances. It wasn't these she was interested in so much as his real friends. It was the latter she wondered when she would get round to meeting. So far he had introduced her to very few.

The house they were going to was a little way out of the city, set in its own grounds. In the dusky light of a fading summer evening it looked a very pleasant place. The parking area in front of it was full of cars, but she didn't think that could account for the tremor of apprehension that went through her. It bewildered her, as well as making her slightly impatient with herself. She had been brought up in a world too similar to this to feel out of place and frightened by it.

Trying to get rid of her inexplicable fears, she walked by Nik's side into the house. He might watch her all evening to see how she acquitted herself, and she didn't want to let him down.

Their hosts were in the hall talking to some of the other guests, but they immediately came forward to speak to them. They were obviously wealthy and cultured people, but even as they approached Vicky wasn't sure she liked them. They almost swarmed over Nik, but they merely looked her coolly up and down, quite different smiles pinned on their faces. The husband stared at Vicky longer than his wife, and with more interest, but he was distracted by something Nik said before she could begin to feel really uncomfortable.

The house was large and ideal for entertaining. Vicky glanced around curiously as she and Nik wandered through the spacious ground-floor rooms. It was a big party and the noise was deafening, with a band playing, and everyone seeming to be laughing and talking at the same time. She saw no one she knew, but as she hadn't expected to that didn't worry her unduly.

She clung closely to Nik's side as he introduced her to a mixed group, but somehow someone came between them and when she looked for him again he had disappeared. Their host, Sir Clive Martin, thrust a glass in her hand and began asking about her engagement. He was very interested in how long she had known Nik and where she lived in London. She tried to answer his questions without making it obvious that she was more interested in where Nik had got to. She wasn't alarmed at first, only rather disappointed when she saw him dancing with another girl. The girl was older than Vicky, nearer his own age, and her hair was too blatantly blonde to be natural. Nevertheless, she was a ravishing creature.

Vicky had thought Nik would have asked her to dance first, and was unaware that the disappointment she tried hard to conceal was reflected in her despondent little face.

Sir Clive, who liked to think he knew all there was to know about women, for once got it right. 'You would like to have danced with Nik yourself,' he murmured smoothly. 'Perhaps you shouldn't have let him get away.'

Vicky tilted her rounded chin courageously. 'He's my fiancée, Sir Clive, but I don't keep him in chains.'

'You may need to, my dear,' he laughed dryly.

Vicky sighed. She knew about men like Sir Clive. She had met a lot of similar types during Vera's reign. They were usually middle-aged and could be extremely malicious. Sir Clive mightn't be quite middle-aged, but he was certainly expert in making sly remarks. And, considering the way his eye was roving, he had little right to criticise other men.

Hearing Vicky sigh gave him an excuse to pat her arm gently. 'I shouldn't take Gilda too much to heart, if I were you, Miss Brown. She has known Nik Demetrious a long time, and he might only be consoling her.'

'Why should he be doing that?' Nicky was unable to prevent herself from asking sharply.

'You can't expect her to be happy over your engagement,' Sir Clive smiled, 'especially when at one time she had high expectations of capturing him herself.'

Vicky was hazily aware of Clive asking her to dance and of her dumb acquiescence. Yet as she automatically circled the floor with him, she was ashamed that she could be so jealous. If Nik wanted to marry Gilda—whoever she was—there had been nothing to stop him. It might not make sense that he was holding her so closely—and Clive seemed determined she should get a good view of them, but Nik was sure to have a good explanation. Uneasily she remembered the redhead at the party in New York and tried not to think of it, or of the way her heart was aching.

The rest of the evening proved a disaster as far as she was concerned. Nik didn't entirely desert her, he danced with her twice, but seemed happy enough to leave her to Sir Clive, who certainly never strayed far from her side. Vicky felt utterly humiliated as she lost count of the times he danced with Gilda, although he never introduced them.

At midnight, when she could stand it no longer, she pleaded to go home. Nik didn't argue, but in the car asked curtly, 'Why so early? Weren't you enjoying yourself?'

How could he ask such a question when he must have

seen how the attention he had poured on Gilda had raised so many spiteful eyebrows? 'It was very nice,' she whispered dully.

'You'll have to show more enthusiasm than that when we entertain, if we get married,' he snapped.

Shouldn't it have been—when we get married? Suddenly, though, Vicky felt too weary to argue with him, and the harder she tried to see the last few hours clearly, the more difficult it became. She had to have time to think. Meanwhile, she had no wish to quarrel with him or say anything which in the morning she might regret.

All the way back to London he scarcely spoke to her and, after dropping her off outside her home, muttered only a brief farewell. He made no attempt to come in or to kiss her goodnight, and she watched his car disappearing along the street with a feeling of overwhelming unhappiness.

During the following days the subtle change in their relationship continued. Vicky tried to ignore it, but she knew it was there. Nik was too busy to lunch with her and she only saw him one evening out of five. This had been to dine at the apartment and some friends of his had also been invited. He pleaded pressure of business even while his tone of voice seemed to indicate he didn't care whether she believed him or not, and although she was aware that he usually took a bulging briefcase home with him she sometimes suspected it was never opened.

A photograph of him dancing at a well known nightclub with a woman she recognised as Gilda confirmed her suspicions that he was seeing someone else, and she trembled that he could be so insensitive. If he wanted to go out with another woman why couldn't he be honest and tell her about it? An engagement could be broken, it wasn't as binding as marriage, and people had made mistakes before. It was Nik's silence she couldn't understand. He was always so forthright about everything, she found it very puzzling that he was being anything but forthright in this instance. Perhaps he was waiting for her to say something, as he must have guessed she was growing suspicious. This Vicky couldn't do. She loved him so much she couldn't think of her pride, but she hoped he would eventually tire of Gilda and come back to her.

It soon became clear that the newspaper photograph had been seen by others, apart from herself, and one girl in particular, who Vicky believed greatly resented her engagement, took a great pleasure in mentioning it to her. In all the departments, Vicky suspected there was increasing gossip, and this hurt terribly. She hadn't thought it was possible to suffer so much, and she often wondered how much longer she could go on.

This question seemed to answer itself when one afternoon she returned to the office and found Gilda with Nik. That morning, apart from work, Nik had ignored her, and she hadn't seen him after work for days. She had had a horrible feeling that things were nearing a climax, and, no matter what she did, she might be unable to avoid it.

It came sooner than she had expected. On returning from lunch, which she had eaten alone, she picked up a pad to go through to Nik's office. She took little notice of the suddenly rather frantic spate of queries her young assistant began throwing at her. Jenny was a nice young girl, but she could be tiresome at times.

'If there's anything you really can't find out for yourself, Jenny,' she said with unusual severity, 'you must ask me later. You know how busy Mr Demetrious is, and I'm already late.'

'I'm sorry, Miss Brown.' Jenny subsided, but looked so anguished that Vicky glanced at her in perplexity.

She soon realised what was worrying Jenny, why she had been so anxious to detain her, when she walked into Nik's office and found Gilda in his arms. As Vicky stood frozen in the doorway, she saw he had his arms tightly around the woman and was kissing her passionately, while Gilda made no attempt to escape. Afterwards Vicky remembered thinking dully that even the cruellest of blows couldn't hurt worse than this.

When, on sensing her presence, Nik raised his head, he didn't appear unduly disturbed. Vicky was amazed that he showed so little emotion. If their positions had been reversed she was sure she would have been shocked to have her fiancé discover her in someone else's arms, but Nik's hard, handsome face was entirely devoid of feeling.

'Miss Becker and I are going out,' he said to Vicky, putting Gilda to one side but keeping hold of her arm. 'I don't know what time I'll be back, but Gordon should be in shortly.'

Miss Becker walked straight past Vicky as though she didn't exist, while Nik only glanced at her once more. Vicky tried to speak, but her throat seemed frozen, like the rest of her, by the look of cold triumph in his eyes as they swept her stricken face.

He didn't return at all that afternoon, and Vicky tried to ignore Gordon's worried glances. He hadn't been in the office when Nik had left, but he must have heard the rumours that were going round. He might easily have bumped into Nik and Gilda as they left, as he had arrived almost immediately afterwards. She was grateful that he didn't express the sympathy he was obviously feeling, but despairing that he thought she was in need of it.

At seven, after reaching home, Vicky could contain herself no longer and rang Nik's apartment. Dion said Mr Demetrious had just come in, but he would get him. While she waited, Vicky distinctly heard a woman's laughter in the background and felt worse than ever.

When, eventually, Nik came to the telephone, he made no apology for keeping her waiting, and when she managed to say, if in a somewhat strangled voice, that she would like to see him, he sounded displeased.

'It's not very convenient.'

'I can come to your place,' she cried in desperation.

'No,' he replied curtly, 'don't do that. I'll come to you, although I can't promise what time it will be.'

It was after ten when Vicky heard his car pulling up outside and she could never remember feeling worse in her life. She knew she had something to do but she loved Nik so much it would be like cutting off a part of herself. Their engagement had become an empty façade which she had to put an end to while she still had a little pride left.

She opened the door when Nik rang. She had been wandering listlessly in the hall and knew it would be him. As he followed her to the lounge she felt icy cold and began to tremble. The past weeks had taken their toll on her; she had lost weight and her face was pale, but her appearance was the last thing she was concerned about at this moment.

In the lounge, as Nik closed the door behind him, she turned to face him. As he approached she thought he looked slightly haggard but as arrogant as ever. She wasn't conscious of studying him closely, she was too busy wondering if he suspected what was coming and was bracing himself for a scene.

'Well?' his voice was silkily belligerent as his eyes swept coolly over her. 'You asked to see me. How long do I have to wait before you tell me what this is all about?'

Vicky felt a rush of suffocating emotion which she tried to stifle. 'I'm sorry if I interrupted your evening with another woman,' she whispered, her voice shaking, despite her attempts to control it.

'She'll forgive me,' he smiled.

Such incredible pain flicked through Vicky that she thought he might have stabbed her. In fact, if he had, it couldn't have hurt as much. Nik was quite unashamedly confessing he was being unfaithful to her. Making a fool of her, she decided bitterly, might be a more appropriate expression!

'Nik,' she took a deep breath, hot tears springing to her eyes, 'it's not easy to say this, but I think the sooner we end our engagement the better.'

She had hoped he might be dismayed, but he merely said, 'Isn't this rather sudden?'

His sarcastic tone caused the threatening tears to overflow, but with a suddenly uncaring hand she wiped them from her cheeks. 'If I'd had any sense I'd have done it days ago.'

Entirely unmoved by her tears, he shrugged indifferently, 'You must please yourself, of course. If that's the way you feel . . .'

'It's not!' she broke in, her blue eyes huge with reproachful anguish. 'I'm not the one who's made a mockery of our engagement. You must realise how the whole office is talking?'

'Don't bore me,' he glared. 'Women always exaggerate.'

'Well, I don't!' Her voice rose hysterically, but she was scarcely aware of it. 'You employ hundreds of people in London alone. You can't pretend you don't know how they hang on your every word and watch everything you do. They never expected our engagement to last; they're laughing at me already.'

'That bothers you most, doesn't it?' he shrugged, but with the glint of satisfaction in his eyes that she had noticed before and still didn't understand.

'No, it doesn't,' she retorted bitterly. 'What bothers me most is the mistake I've made. I thought you loved me!'

'Have I ever said so?'

Hating the way he parried with her so coolly, Vicky abjectly shook her head.

'Or asked you to meet my family?'

She was being torn in two by his questions and the sudden change in his manner which hinted at barely concealed fury. Again, because her throat was choked up, she shook her head.

'Didn't you ever wonder why I never told you I loved

you?' he pressed on, she thought in the manner of a public prosecutor.

'I believed it must have something to do with the customs of your country,' she whispered, as he obviously expected an answer. 'I thought you loved me, because of . . .'

'Yes?' he prompted as she paused in confusion.

'Because of the way you kissed me,' she said defiantly but unable to look at him.

She could almost feel him studying the wild flush on her cheeks, but he wasn't answering questions, he was asking them. 'And my family?'

Feeling driven, she replied wearily, 'I didn't even know you had a family, but does it matter? You know as well as I do there's nothing left between us. It's all finished.'

She was weeping openly now, and his mouth curled derisively. 'You're finding it hurts?'

'I loved you,' she sobbed, trying to control herself as she pulled off her engagement ring.

That he accepted it immediately, thrusting it into his pocket with scarcely a glance, seemed the final blow. She had treasured her little ring, woven such dreams round it, which had all come to nothing.

In the short silence that followed she had vague hopes that Nik might ask her to forgive him and start again, but he did no such thing. Dully she asked, 'Why did you ask me to marry you in the first place?'

'Revenge,' he drawled, very softly.

She was reminded of the sibilant hiss of a king cobra. 'Revenge?' She was completely bewildered.

'You heard,' his eyes smouldered as he decided she was being deliberately obtuse. 'You imagined I'd be as easy to dupe as my uncle? He nearly died because of you, but I'm afraid I'm made of rather different material.'

Vicky stared at him, unable to believe she was hearing properly. 'What are you saying?' she gasped.

'You may as well give up,' he snapped. 'The time is past for pretending.'

'I'm not pretending anything!' unless it's that I'm not going slightly mad, Vicky thought desperately. 'You'll have to explain.'

'As you like,' he snarled savagely, 'but you'll pay dearly for every word I have to spell out. You did irreparable damage to my family and it was a shock to discover I was actually harbouring the viper myself, but the proof was indisputable.' As Vicky gazed at him in mounting horror, he continued harshly, 'My first impulse was to throw you out, or maybe kill you before you tried to destroy someone else. Then I decided it would be too easy for you, you deserved to suffer first.'

'Suffer?' Vicky stammered, trying to gather sufficient wit to understand what he was talking about. Whatever he was trying to say it must make sense, because whatever else Nik Demetrious was, he wasn't stupid. Yet neither was she! But she had never heard of his uncle and, as far as she knew, she had never made anyone suffer.

Nik's eyes flicked contemptuously over her pale, tear-streaked face, discounting her tortured expression. 'When I asked you to be my secretary, you must have thought I had played right into your hands. You decided I was a better bet than my uncle, but you didn't expect to fall in love with me. That was where I scored. I knew I had you in my power when I realised you were attracted to me, and if I've managed to break your mercenary little heart and humiliate you, so much the better. It's a lesson you badly needed. Somehow I don't think you'll be so keen to play with any man's affections again.'

Vicky swayed as the room reeled around her. 'Nik,' she pleaded, 'won't you believe I still have no idea what you're talking about.'

'No, I won't,' he ground out between clenched teeth,

'and if you go on pretending ignorance much longer, heaven help me, I'll hit you!'

Because the fury in his eyes suggested he wouldn't hesitate, Vicky found enough sense to whisper frantically, 'You must have mistaken me for someone else!'

'No, I haven't,' he said grimly. 'I made very sure of that. I checked and double-checked. You were in Corfu,' he named dates and she was forced to nod. 'There can't be two fair-headed Vicky Browns, living in London, working for my firm. There aren't—I made sure of that. In three weeks you contrived to get my sixty-year-old uncle so besotted that, after you'd promised to marry him, he gave you a large sum of money—which enabled you to buy this house! You even boasted that it was a present.

'But after this money had been safely transferred to your bank, you sent him a charming little note saying you didn't love him any more. You had made a mistake, you said, and were going to marry someone else. According to my aunt, my uncle's sister, you left the island overnight and simply disappeared. My uncle might have come after you, but not when you were going to marry another man. Instead he tried to commit suicide. If I hadn't arrived in time there would have been no hope for him.'

CHAPTER SIX

'I STILL say you're making a mistake!' Vicky cried, almost incoherent with shock. 'That wasn't me, it couldn't have been. I've never met your uncle. I don't even know his name.'

'Stop lying to me!' Nik suddenly reached out to shake her viciously. 'You may have thought you were on a good thing, swindling old men out of their money, but I'm going to see that you don't make a career of it. The authorities are often very interested in women like you!'

'You can't be serious?' she gasped.

'We'll see,' he grunted non-committally, 'For a start this house will be sold and the money returned to Philip.'

Again Vicky tried to protest, but when Nik finished shaking her she had no clear idea of what she was saying. 'How many times do I have to tell you I never knew your uncle? And if I had been guilty of everything you accuse me of, would it be any more despicable than what you've done to me? You never had any intention of marrying me—it was merely an act to deceive me all these weeks. You—you kissed me, let me fall in love with you, all in cold blood. I don't know how you could have done such a thing!'

'I'm going to do more than that,' he retorted harshly. 'I'm going to enjoy watching everyone laughing at you while you reap the rewards of your duplicity.'

'I won't be coming back,' she whispered, knowing it would be impossible.

'Oh, yes, you will, you cheating little bitch,' he said softly. 'You signed a contract for a year, remember, and I intend holding you to it. You're going to suffer and suffer again. It will be a lesson you won't ever forget.'

96

Vicky stared at him, feeling completely helpless. She didn't know how to convince him of her innocence. The story he had told her was tragic and he couldn't have made it up. She had been to Corfu and the girl he mentioned answered her description so exactly it was incredible, so how was she to convince him he had made a mistake?

Unevenly she cried, 'I can only keep repeating, Nik, that I never knew your uncle. You must have been given the wrong information.'

At her continuing defiance, his face hardened while his eyes glittered with fury. 'You haven't even the courage to make a honest confession!'

'Because I haven't one to make!' she insisted.

For an answer, his face hardened, becoming ugly and sneering as she shrank back, he exclaimed harshly, 'You will stay with me until you're ready to make a full confession. Only when you do this, and go on your knees begging my forgiveness, might I let you go.'

'Please, Nik,' she moaned dizzily, because she didn't think she could survive working for him, 'don't make me!'

'I can and I will,' he promised coldly, 'You showed no mercy for one of my family, so don't begin complaining like a spineless coward when I can find none for you.'

The next week proved a complete torment for Vicky. There were times when she didn't think she could go on. Nik forced her to continue working for him. The morning after he had taken his ring back and made such terrible accusations, she hadn't gone to the office until he rang and threatened terrifying things if she didn't turn up within the hour.

She had made it with only minutes to spare, and, minus her ring, it wasn't long before the news of her broken engagement spread through the entire building like wildfire. She was humiliated continually, and Nik was so determined she should suffer that he became the worst offender of them all. She wasn't to know that the sight of her slight figure, her bruised blue eyes, haunting with their expression of hunted innocence, was driving him slowly to madness.

After work Vicky spent long hours attempting to unravel the mystery of her mistaken identity, but failed. Someone had used her name, that was obvious, but she had no idea why. It didn't really make sense as, according to Nik, this girl and his uncle had met accidentally, so nothing could have been prearranged. What she found most puzzling was the odd conviction she couldn't get rid of that what had happened on Corfu did have something to do with her. Yet the more she worried over it the more her mind seemed to come up against a blank wall.

Nik's brutal treatment and his lack of faith in her hurt most of all, but there didn't seem to be anything she could do about it. The harder she denied ever knowing his uncle, the more infuriated he became. Every day he taunted her about it, asking if she was ready to talk, and she sensed his growing anger when she stubbornly continued to shake her head.

He hadn't said anything more about the house, and she thought he had forgotten about it until he asked her to stay late one evening. Vicky didn't mind working overtime, she was used to it, and anything was better than going home and spending the evening in misery. Not that she wept any more. All her tears seemed to have dried up, or were perhaps as frozen as her heart. Mercifully something had snapped and she no longer knew the extreme anguish which had often become almost unbearable. If she was back on the emotionless plane where she had been for years, she wasn't complaining. Nik Demetrious had taken her love and flung it back in her face. Her one prayer now was that she would never be so vulnerable again.

She was thankful that now she could watch Nik dully without feeling anything when, instead of getting on

with the business he had said was so important, he
raised his dark head from the paper he was studying to
renew his attack on her about his uncle. She knew he
wasn't pleased when, instead of being reduced almost to
tears, her eyes went curiously blank.

'I'd rather you didn't say anything while Gordon is
still around,' she said coolly.

Gordon had been a tower of strength, accepting that
she needed help and giving it in various unobtrusive
ways without asking questions, and she had no desire
for him to overhear the harsh accusations Nik
continued to pour on her. Gordon appeared to believe
she and Nik had quarrelled over something trivial, and
she would rather he didn't know the truth.

Nik's eyes speared into her as he cursed, none too
silently, under his breath. 'He's gone home. Are you
blind now as well as deaf?'

The insolence in his narrowed grey eyes was
unbearable. Vicky shivered but remained resolute. 'I'm
neither, but I wish I were deaf sometimes, when you go
on about your precious uncle.'

'Do you, indeed!' His voice was full of leashed fury.
When she lowered her gaze, a little frightened at her
own impulsive temerity, he got up to come round his
desk and stand beside her. Before she realised what he
was doing he had grabbed a handful of her thick, silky
hair.

'Look at me when I speak to you, damn you!' he
snapped, deliberately using his hold on her hair to draw
her head back.

He had never been as near for weeks and he was
staring at the shadows and bruises, her new extreme
thinness, as though she disgusted him.

'You deserve it,' he muttered savagely.

Sensation was shooting from his fingers which she
didn't like. Like his tongue, they were searing her with
fire.

He stared down at her, as if he was actually trying to

see what lay behind the apprehensive blue eyes widening under his.

'I'm going to put the house up for sale,' he said curtly. 'You can hand over the deeds and I'll decide the best way to do it.'

'No!' Vicky was so shocked she jerked away from him so quickly it must have brought some of her hair out by the roots. Wincing with pain, she tried to tell herself he was bluffing, but it was another thing believing it. He was capable of anything, she should think, if he put his mind to it! 'You can't do that!' she cried, suddenly as angry as he was. 'Can't you understand I didn't have anything to do with what happened to your uncle?'

'No, I can't,' he threw back furiously. 'And there's one way to prove it. I'm taking you to Corfu, then we shall see who's bluffing?'

'Oh, no!' Vicky's eyes darkened with horror. This was worse than anything she could have envisaged. She couldn't bear to think of going to Greece with Nik. She hated him, but that disturbed her almost as much as loving him had done. It was inexplicable, but it seemed an emotion just as capable of tearing her in two. For a moment she was tempted to fall on her hands and knees, as he wanted her to, and confess to anything, even if it was something she wasn't guilty of.

'Doesn't your very reluctance prove your guilt?' he asked, so contemptuously it immediately disallowed such an easy way out.

'No, it doesn't!' she denied sharply. 'It's you who's trying to do that, by fair means or foul. You're determined to prove me guilty of everything you've accused me of. Your pride obviously won't let you rest until you do.'

'I could kill you for that!' Nik looked so incensed she thought he might enjoy it too.

'There's a first time for everything,' she cried recklessly, feeling dead inside because of what he had already done to her.

'What the hell do you mean?'

The savage note in his voice might have intimidated her if she hadn't been past caring. 'You could be wrong,' she suggested flatly. 'You've never been before, have you? As the great Nik Demetrious you really believe you're as infallible as one of your famous Greek gods!'

His eyes smouldered so darkly she had to look away, but when he replied it was merely to agree coldly. 'Facts speak for themselves, Miss Brown. I don't have to rely on the influence of mythology. If I didn't get my facts right I wouldn't be where I am today.'

Such supreme confidence demolished Vicky's common sense, making her rashly impetuous. 'I'll prove you aren't right this time,' she exclaimed, anger again breaking though the inertia that had enclosed her for days. 'I'll come to Corfu with you, Mr Demetrious, as soon as you like!'

She was still regretting her rashness, a few days later, as the plane bringing them from Athens circled over the hilly forests and blue waters of Corfu, prior to landing. Almost all the bravado she had shown in Nik's office had gone and she knew only a shivering apprehension. If Nik hadn't been sure of her guilt would he have brought her here? It was this certainty of his which was beginning to make her doubt her own sanity. She found she was asking herself if it was possible that she could be the girl who had deceived his uncle, and only by reassuring herself continually was she able to go on.

Nik was sitting by her side looking as big and arrogant as ever and completely bored. Their air hostess seemed to have seldom taken her eyes off him, but he had been quite unresponsive to such attention. Vicky had been surprised that he had chosen to travel by public transport until he had told her that one of his helicopters was already on the island and it was senseless to bring another. They would use this when they returned to the mainland.

He had continued to abuse her continually during their brief sojourn in Athens, though, mercifully, she had seen little of him. Miss Devlin, looking superbly fit, had taken over, while Vicky was dismissed and told to rest in Nik's superb penthouse at the top of the huge warren of modern offices. She didn't know how he'd explained her presence to Miss Devlin and she hadn't learnt whether the news of their engagement, and the ending of it had reached this far. Miss Devlin had merely glanced at her closely and not asked any questions.

Vicky, unable to rest with her uneasy thoughts, would have liked to wander outside, but Nik had forbidden it. As they were leaving in the morning, he said, it wouldn't be worth the effort.

She had only seen him at dinner which, not unexpectedly, finished in a blazing row. It frequently bewildered Vicky that he could raise his voice to her so harshly when he never lost his temper with anyone else. Whenever he was infuriated with others he was always cool and in control.

During the main courses, served, she thought, by too many servants, he had ignored her apart from seeing she had everything she needed. This was innate courtesy, born in him, she realised, nothing to do with her personally at all. It had been over coffee, when they had been alone, that he had brought up the surprising question of her innocence.

'It astounds me that you are still untouched.'

Vicky had flushed, quick to realise she was under some kind of attack but not quite sure how to defend herself. She was too familiar with Nik's cutting contempt to imagine he was conveying any kind of compliment and she distrusted the cold glitter in his eyes as they wandered insolently over her simple but effective dress.

'Can't you answer my question?' he snapped.

'I wasn't aware it was one.' She had looked away, hoping he wouldn't notice her hot cheeks. 'It—it's not a usual topic for after-dinner conversation.'

'I want to know!'

This time she didn't pretend to misunderstand, and she knew he would insist until she answered. She might leave him and go to bed, but he would probably only begin at breakfast.

'It's not something I've ever thought about,' she confessed stiffly. 'I just like being as I am. It has its advantages.'

She wasn't quite sure what she meant herself, but she was quite unprepared for the savage lecture that followed.

'Girls like you are worse than common prostitutes,' he had finished, adding, as he jumped to his feet and strode out, 'Innocence is no longer a thing to be revered when it is used merely to taunt a man and drive him to his death.'

'I can't promise how Philip will react when he sees you again,' Nik murmured in her ear after they had come down and were leaving the airport in his helicopter. They were sitting behind the pilot so he couldn't hear, but Vicky wished Nik hadn't mentioned it immediately. His voice went on relentlessly, as though he didn't intend giving her nerves any respite. 'On the surface we're a pretty civilised lot, but underneath, the old passions of our race still run fairly deep.'

Vicky didn't need to be told that. He had denied the vendetta, but hadn't she ample evidence that he supported it? And she had always felt a certain violence in his kisses. Now she understood the hatred which had been driving him, but she hadn't then. She had been nervous of him and alarmed that her body responded so wantonly and blindly. It gave her a sense of satisfaction that she could think of being in Nik's arms now with scarcely a quiver.

'Are we going to your uncle's house straight away?' she asked hesitantly. No matter how innocent she was she couldn't help feeling slightly sick at the prospect of having to meet an elderly man who had apparently suffered very badly. And the element of mystery she had sensed in London still lingered, making her doubly reluctant to meet him for fear of what she might discover. She wished repeatedly that she hadn't allowed herself to be provoked by anger into coming here with Nik.

Their departure from London had been hurried. Once she had agreed to come to Greece with him, he hadn't given her a chance to change her mind. Appointments were cancelled, work relegated, appropriate arrangements made. Gordon had been left behind, something she knew he had taken as a hopeful sign that the quarrel between Nik and herself would be patched up while they were away. He hadn't said so, but it was obvious that he believed this was why Nik was taking her off on her own.

At the end of an exhausting few days Vicky realised she had seen or heard nothing of Gilda Becker, but she wasn't surprised when she rang up and asked to speak to Nik.

Vicky was depressed to notice how much her hand was shaking as she put her through. It puzzled her when she felt so frozen inside. She had no idea what he said to Gilda, but she could be under no misapprehension as to what he said to her.

'Never do that again without consulting me first,' he had thrown at her furiously, leaving her to think what she liked as he slammed out. Vicky had felt too bewildered and startled to do anything but stare after him dumbly, but she did wonder if he had been using Gilda merely to serve his own diabolical ends and now had no further use for her.

They were making rapid progress across the island, which she could see was beautiful. It was strange that she couldn't look at it without shivering. Nik hadn't answered her query and she asked again, thinking he hadn't heard.

'No,' he said curtly, and she glanced at him quickly. His roughly hewn features were paler than usual, there could be no mistaking his grimness. 'We will go and see Philip in the morning.'

For a moment she thought he was considering her until he added, 'I have to make sure he is well first.'

Vicky sighed. He must be meaning to assess the degree of shock his uncle could withstand, but she only knew a great urge to get the ordeal over.

On hearing her sigh, Nik must have guessed at what was passing through her mind, for he advised harshly, 'It won't do you any harm to wait a little longer. You had better get a good night's sleep, because after Philip is through with you it might be a long time before you sleep again!'

Vicky gazed from the helicopter blindly, the long sandy shores and blue seas of the island swimming before her unhappy eyes. The heat was blistering, but the landscape remained green, even luxuriant, and the backdrop of mountains and distant vistas was almost as wonderful as the gorgeous beaches and magnificent coastline. She had loved it here when she had been on holiday, but this trip would be entirely different. She had no illusions about this. Regardless of the outcome, she knew instinctively she was going to suffer. If not in the way Nik had envisaged, she was aware there were many different kinds of torture, some of which she might not be able to endure. When a coldness came over her, despite the heat, Nik asked sharply why she was trembling.

'You wouldn't understand,' she muttered, trying to sit still.

He looked as if he would liked to have shaken her again. 'I think I do,' his eyes glittered, 'but you only have yourself to blame.'

'You're the one who's in for a shock,' she retorted unevenly, but he merely stared at her, his mouth curling disbelievingly.

His villa was a pleasant place without being impressive. Somehow Vicky had imagined it would be quite different. It was set almost on the beach, and the beach was private, he assured her. No one came here, although the big hotels were encroaching fast. One day, he shrugged, it might be time to move on.

There were servants at the villa, but not nearly as many as he had in Athens. A Greek couple saw to the house and gardens, along with a young maid who seemed to be forever running to and fro.

Nik introduced Vicky briefly as his secretary and they appeared to accept her as such. The housekeeper's name was Daphne, while her husband's was Cyprian, and the little maid was called Delta. Vicky wondered if these would be the last of his various households she would meet before he let her go.

The villa was plainly furnished but cool and very spacious. The gardens and views around it were so exciting that Vicky doubted if anyone would want to stay indoors very long, but the big lounge was extremely comfortable and she could imagine that in October, when the thunderstorms came, after the long, hot summer, that with a log fire burning and plenty of books to read it would be beautifully cosy.

'I'm going out,' said Nik, as Daphne was about to show her to her room. 'If I'm not back you will be served dinner, but on no account leave the villa or go down to the sea. If you're tempted to swim you'll find a pool in the grounds.'

She didn't see him again until late that evening. When he returned she was just about to go to bed. As she had spent a terrible day alone with her thoughts, the face she turned to him was strained and colourless.

If Nik Demetrious didn't look much better, she felt

too distraught to notice. 'I hope you've had a good day,' she emphasised bitterly.

He regarded her in cold anger. 'Not even you could say that talking to a man who still feels sore and humiliated is enjoyable.'

'Your uncle?'

'Who else? If you insist on calling him that. Why not Philip? I don't think you were so reticent a few months back.'

'It's not my fault that he feels so bad,' she retorted, her nerves in a worse state than she'd imagined. 'I suppose you believe what you're doing for him is going to help?'

'It's all I can do,' Nik replied curtly.

Recklessly she cried, 'You think seeing me will mend his broken heart? If I had been the girl he was engaged to and he really loved her, wouldn't it make him feel worse?'

'You are that girl, damn you, and it was to make you admit it as well as to shock Philip to his senses that I brought you here.' The taut line of his mouth gave way to a thin, cruel smile as he paused. 'I intended taking you to him exactly as you are, but I see now how that could be a mistake.'

Vicky stared at him, her soft lips trembling with uncertainty as his eyes wandered insolently over her, the sudden grasp of his hand on her waist almost as cruel as his expression. The servants had gone; they didn't apparently sleep in the villa. Fright licked through her as she realised just how isolated she was here with Nik.

Allowing his words time to sink in, Nik continued suavely, 'How much better Philip might feel if I presented him with a poor, broken creature, instead of one looking pathetically like a misunderstood angel. The latter might only appeal to his ever-ready sympathy. If you spent the night with me I would make very sure that no one would mistake you for anything else but what you really are. And, believe me, nothing cools a man's blood quicker than the sight of soiled goods!'

As his mouth moved towards her she whispered, 'No!' in a shocked gasp and turned her head away. She tried to evade him, but as soon as she felt his warm, moist breath on her cheeks she knew she was lost. There was no way she could combat his superior strength or reason with the obviously maddened trend of his thoughts. The frantic turning and twisting of her head availed her nothing. Her chin was caught in an iron band to hold her still while his mouth found its helpless target.

Her lips were crushed and bruised, rendered numb beneath his savage assault. More pain shot through her as she attempted to free an arm to hit him and he twisted it behind her back, keeping it there in the hand which held her tightly against him. The blood rushed to her ears while her pulses thundered.

Fear such as she had never known before ripped through her as he raised his head to ask if she'd had enough. 'More than enough!' she almost spat at him.

Her contempt drove him to fury. 'You treat Philip like dirt—you'd like to treat me the same way. Are you surprised that I'm driven to teach you a lesson?'

'You'll regret it!' she cried, praying frantically for the right words to disperse his anger.

'No, I won't,' he snarled, his dark features satanic. 'I was a fool not to think of it before. You're probably planning to hoodwink Philip again! You'll go to him, all sweet innocence, complaining how I've been beating you up!'

'You must be insane!' she said hoarsely, almost believing it.

'No,' he mocked coldly, 'I'm just beginning to come to my senses. I'm going to make very sure he doesn't want you.'

'I'll hate you!' she whispered, her blue eyes full of fear and despair. 'Don't you care?'

'You flatter yourself, lady,' he jeered, eyes smouldering as he began kissing her again. 'Why should I care? But I can promise you won't hate me.'

When the ruthless line of his mouth clamped down on hers, Vicky's lips parted and to her horror she found her resistance melting. A fiery sensation invaded her and she found herself submitting to the caressing hands that unzipped her dress and began wandering over her smooth, warm skin. As the fight died slowly out of her an uncontrollable shudder shook her. The world tilted dangerously as his fingers pressed urgently into her flesh, exploring her slender body. With a moan of ecstasy she clung to him, giving him back kiss for kiss, and, as passion surged violently between them, her arms went tightly around his neck.

Just as Nik picked her up, his intentions unmistakable, the telephone rang. Abruptly he hesitated, as if he would have liked to ignore it, then with a smothered exclamation he put her down again. 'Philip said he would ring,' he muttered. 'There's some information I promised to look up for him. If I don't answer he will keep trying until I do.'

Vicky stumbled away.

'Don't move,' he commanded.

She waited until he was talking to his uncle, then fled. There was a heavy lock on the door of her room and she hoped he couldn't get in. The window was open, she secured this too, praying it would hold. Dear heaven, she prayed, collapsing on her bed, please keep him away!

She scarcely slept, but she never heard a sound all night, and when dawn came silently she shivered with relief. She didn't learn why Nik had changed his mind until they were having breakfast.

'I didn't think you were worth breaking a door down for,' he said contemptuously, as she tried to swallow a few mouthfuls of coffee before they left to see his uncle. 'I've decided to rely on Philip's good sense.'

Vicky was wearing a cool, sleeveless little dress in

blue cotton which didn't seem to please him. 'Can't you find something with a jacket, perhaps, instead of flaunting yourself like that?'

His lips curled back from his white teeth in a snarl and as their eyes met Vicky looked away. She went obediently to fetch a cardigan, but refused to change her dress. Nik noted this grimly but made no further comment.

She tried not to notice his appearance and wished her mind wasn't so full of clear-cut pictures of him whenever she closed her eyes. Nik, as she had first met him, sitting at his desk, his powerful body relaxed but his eyes not missing a thing. Nik, in New York, just as dynamically alert but kinder to her, dancing with her, making love to her. Vicky's breath caught as physically and mentally he imposed himself on her. Wearily she wished she could get rid of his tough, handsome image. It was something she could do without, especially now that she hated him.

'How do you know your uncle wants to see me? she asked, as they drove over rough minor roads in a four-wheel-drive vehicle capable of going anywhere.

He rammed a gear savagely. 'Wouldn't you want to see someone who had jilted you and done you out of a great deal of money? You're going to assure him he will get it back—every penny!'

Nik was in a foul mood. Her heart beating heavily, she said bitterly, 'Your family mustn't receive ill-treatment, it seems, only dish it out!'

'What the hell are you getting at now?'

Out of the corner of her eye, his hands tightened threateningly on the steering wheel, but she ploughed on regardless. 'I shouldn't need to explain. You promised to marry me and changed your mind.'

'That was different,' he gritted. 'That was done to serve a specific purpose.'

'I realise that now,' she retorted, 'but it was cheating all the same. I thought you loved me.'

'You can disabuse yourself of that idea immediately,' he laughed harshly.

She could see his mouth twisting in an angry sneer. 'The idea no longer appeals to me,' she said sharply. 'I wouldn't have your love now on a silver salver.'

'I've told you before, it's other people you should be feeling sorry for, not yourself. Stop pretending you're young and innocent!'

She shrank from the glittering darkness of his eyes, the piercing anger and contempt in them. 'I am young,' she whispered, having a idiotic desire to convince him of something. 'I'm twenty-two.'

He glanced at her again, sharply. 'I intend having that checked,' he told her. 'I've reason to think you're older than we've been led to believe.'

Was there anything he hadn't thought of? 'When it comes to lying and cheating, in your estimation I must be due a gold medal!'

'Which you'd probably cash.'

Vicky fell silent. It was futile to argue with him. His opinion of her couldn't be worse and was firmly fixed; nothing she said was going to change it. She wondered what form his remorse would take when they saw his uncle, but even if he went down on his knees and apologised it wouldn't make any difference. She despised him, and nothing was going to alter that. Her confusing response to his kisses the night before, she put out of her mind. People could respond to each other without love, it was merely some sort of chemical reaction.

It was a beautiful morning. Vicky let her eyes wander. Corfu was a beautiful island, she wished she could have known it before the tourists—of which she admitted to being one—arrived. She would rather gaze at the sea and the trees on the hillside than at the big hotels.

Everywhere there was an amazing variety of trees; oak, laurel, orange, heath, cypress, lemon, horse-chestnut; she lost count while counting them as they drove by. She was surprised she could see anything but the ordeal ahead of her, for she was taut with apprehension. The mind was incredible. It could both protect and crucify. It could raise one to incredible heights, then hit one with a passing thought capable of bringing one crashing unhappily to earth again. It had known the strain she was under and offered as a brief diversion the trees on the roadside. Unfortunately she couldn't forget for long that somewhere along this road was a man who Nik fully expected would denounce her, and for the first time since arriving here, Vicky wondered if she would be able to prove her innocence. Amazingly, it had only just occurred to her that, somewhere, she might have a double.

It took them half an hour to reach Philip's villa. It wasn't nearly so isolated as Nik's and the twice the size. The only word Vicky could find to describe it was impressive. She stared, in dull appreciation, at the ornamental gardens, paved and terraced right down to the sea which lapped a stone jetty against which a smart yacht was moored.

The yacht was white, the sea blue, the sky above it dazzling. The whole scene was impressive. If he owned all this, a girl might easily jump to the conclusion that Philip Demetrious was a millionaire!

As Nik drew up under the shelter of green, overhanging trees, he said abruptly, 'Philip is alone. His sister, who I realise you must have met, is out. I made sure of this as I wished to spare him too much humiliation.'

'Of course,' Vicky steadied trembling legs and managed to nod coolly. 'I hope your uncle appreciates how you think of everything.'

'You're beyond belief!' he bit out furiously.

She knew she was getting under his skin as his voice rasped between clenched teeth, but she didn't think he had any reason to look so pale. After all, the whole purpose of this trip was to establish her guilt, to prove

her a liar and restore his uncle to his right senses again.
Where was his usual watertight confidence? Where was
the self-satisfied gleam of a man congratulating himself
on duty well done? She stared at him, noticing his
haggard face, and wondered.

They walked to the house without speaking. A
manservant was waiting to usher them to the lounge.
Out of the heat, the tiled and marbled entrance hall
beckoned coolly. Vicky would liked to have lingered
there, but Nik's hand drew her relentlessly on. Despite
knowing she had nothing to fear, her heart beat so
rapidly she thought he must hear it. The dreadful
feeling of premonition which she had known for days
returned and for a moment she thought wildly of
running, but Nik, as though sensing this, tightened his
grip on her arm.

'Oh, no, you don't!' he snapped, thrusting her
savagely into his uncle's presence.

CHAPTER SEVEN

PHILIP DEMETRIOUS was a short, grey-haired man bearing little resemblance to his nephew. He looked about sixty, and Vicky could detect in him the tiredness of someone under considerable strain. He was obviously expecting his nephew, but he glanced at Vicky with a faint frown. When she saw it she stiffened, for one incredulous moment believing he meant to denounce her.

Nik, aware of her reaction, drew her relentlessly forward. A brief glimpse of his face as she hung back revealed a beading of perspiration. He must be anxious about his uncle and bracing himself for what was to come.

Philip merely switched his faded eyes from Vicky to him and said, 'You didn't say you were bringing a young lady with you. At least I don't think you did.'

Nik frowned blackly as Philip glanced at Vicky again. His expression was kindly but showed only polite interest, nothing more. 'You don't have to pretend, Philip,' he said harshly.

Philip's bushy brows drew together as though he found Nik's attitude reprehensible. 'Pretend what, Nik? I can't say I've been over enamoured with blondes since—well, you know what I'm referring to, but it would scarcely be fair to allow such an incident, regrettable though it was, to prejudice me against every fair young woman.'

Nik looked stunned, while Vicky trembled. Without giving herself time to think, she spoke quickly to Philip. 'I'm sorry, Mr Demetrious, but Nik believes I'm the—the girl you fell in love with a few months ago.'

Tersely Nik intervened. 'I don't know if you've been

in touch, arranged something between you, but it's no use pretending to me you don't know each other.'

It was clear that Philip was taken aback. Before Nik's sharp attack he went quite pale. Nevertheless he drew himself up with a certain dignity Vicky had to admire.

'I'm not pretending anything, Nik. This is the first time I've ever set eyes on this young lady—whom,' he rebuked his nephew silently with a dry glance, 'you haven't introduced me to yet.'

'There can't be two Vicky Browns!'

Philip's head jerked up. He was visibly startled. 'What did you say, Nik?'

'You heard,' Nik looked as if he had stood just about enough. 'This is Vicky Brown, who works as a secretary for the Demetrious Shipping Lines in London.'

Philip swayed and sat down with a muttered excuse. Vicky noticed with alarm how he suddenly shook. 'It must be a coincidence,' he quavered.

Why didn't Nik get him a drink? Anyone could see he needed one. 'He won't believe me,' she said tensely, when Nik didn't move.

'Nik,' Philip suddenly squared his drooping shoulders, glancing up resolutely, 'I have a photograph. I didn't show it to you before because after my accident I was too ill. A friend of mine took it. The other Vicky—my Vicky, I mean—didn't like having her photograph taken, but Will had some kind of hidden camera. He had the film developed and sent it to me the day before she went and I had to hide it for fear she destroyed it. I meant to destroy it myself afterwards but somehow never found the courage. As a matter of fact I'm glad I didn't, because I find I can look at it now without a quiver. I find I'm cured,' he laughed cynically. 'An odd confession for a man to make when he declared he never would be, but it's true.'

As they watched he rose, taking a key from his pocket as he paused by a locked drawer. From it he extracted a large photograph and showed it to them. He actually gave it to Nik, but as Vicky was standing close to him she couldn't help seeing it too. Immediately she felt herself going cold with horror as she glanced at it and found her stepmother's face staring back at her.

Vicky was still in shock when they returned to Nik's villa. Vera's true identity had been established beyond doubt. The photograph was quite conclusive. It revealed the similarity in colouring that had obviously confused Nik, but the differences were unmistakable. Vera's eyes were brown, for instance, and her mouth was small, while Vicky's was soft and wide. Even the shape of their noses was different, and it was easy to see that Vera was older. If Nik still didn't believe, his uncle had said, he had only to wait until his sister returned and she would verify that Vicky and the girl he had been engaged to were two entirely different people.

Vicky had told him, her voice trembling, that she had wedding photographs at home if any further proof was needed that Vera was her stepmother, but Philip had shaken his head. Vera had apparently used Vicky's name, as it wâs so near her own, in order to pose as a single girl, and her job to get an introduction to Philip Demetrious. How she had even been aware of his existence was a mystery to Vicky, but Vera had known countless people and been extremely cunning.

Whatever Vicky had expected it had never been this. The shock had unnerved her, although she had tried to pull herself together sufficiently to explain a little about Vera. Philip had been kind and understanding, however, in refusing to allow her to give more than brief details. Bitterly Vicky wondered if, in different ways, Vera was going to haunt her for ever.

If she had received a shock, Nik appeared to have suffered one too. Philip, stricken by further evidence of Vera's amazing duplicity, might have failed to notice it, but Vicky had. Nik had admittedly looked grim before they had left his house that morning, but as they returned his eyes were considerably darker and deep lines edged the corners of his tightly clamped mouth.

'It was kind of your uncle to offer us lunch,' Vicky said stiffly, 'but I wasn't hungry. I still couldn't eat anything,' she insisted, as they entered the villa and she feared he was about to order lunch immediately.

He surprised her by replying, 'Neither could I, but I think you should have some coffee, and a drink, perhaps.'

'I'd really rather go to my room,' she replied.

Nik was silent for a moment and her tension mounted. When he did speak there was a note in his voice that she couldn't define. He wasn't sharp yet he sounded strangely on edge. 'We have to talk, Vicky, you know that. Staying in your room isn't going to solve anything. I don't think you'd even be able to rest, and I certainly shan't.'

'I'd be away from you.' Her long, curling lashes swept her cheeks, then lifted as she stared at him defiantly.

'I deserved that.' Grimly he turned from her to order a light meal from Daphne. As the woman smiled and disappeared, he added, 'You may go and freshen up, but be back in five minutes.'

Feeling sick, Vicky rinsed her hot face and hands in cold water. Nik was stunned that he had been proved wrong, if for just once in a lifetime. Because of his pride she was obviously going to receive an apology, but she knew he was also curious. That must be why he wanted to detain her. At his uncle's villa, a lot had been glossed over to spare Philip's feelings. While Philip had protested, Nik, with a skill she had frequently watched in boardrooms, had kept her halting sentences to the minimum. He had only allowed her to say how her father had remarried when she was twelve and Vera ten years older. How, as soon as she had finished boarding school at eighteen and found a job, her father had died and she had gone to live in digs and hadn't seen Vera since. He had stared at her in grim silence while she had tried to explain briefly about her father's house; the letter she had received from Vera after she had married again. But when Philip had asked, she had had to confess she had no idea who Vera had married, or where she was living.

As she dried herself, Vicky suspected that despite Philip's avowals, some of the pain of Vera's desertion still lingered. She wondered what he had thought of her and sensed that, despite Vera, he had liked her. As they had left, he had told Nik to bring her for a meal the next day, so she could meet his sister.

Hurriedly Vicky combed her hair, without giving it a great deal of attention. Nik would be waiting for her to fill in all the gaps and she hoped to be able to persuade him that that wasn't necessary. All she wanted to do now was to return home and forget everything.

As soon as he heard her coming, Nik stopped prowling around the lounge to usher her to a seat. In front of it, on a low table, was a large tray of food. The aroma from the coffee pot was tantalising, but she gazed at the food without interest.

Leaving her, Nik returned quickly, holding a glass. Vicky kept her eyes averted but knew he was standing beside her. He put the glass, full of an amber liquid, in her hand. 'Drink this up,' he said firmly.

Forcing herself to remain calm, she turned to look at him. Meeting his dark eyes, she saw the tension in them and felt curiously numb. At the same time she found herself wishing illogically that he wasn't so compellingly handsome. In her absence he had thrown off the light jacket he had been wearing and his black trousers fitted tautly over his strong thighs, while his half open shirt revealed a wealth of dark, curling hair. She remembered how it had felt to be crushed against it and took a quick gulp of her drink.

He sat down beside her, his arm along the back of the couch. After watching a little colour stealing to her pale cheeks, he relaxed slightly. His first words were not unexpected.

'I owe you an apology.'

Vicky tensed. 'Why not just say you admit to being wrong? I'm sure you don't really feel sorry.'

Some of the arrogance went out of his manner as he retorted tightly. 'I am sorry, Vicky. You must allow me to know my own feelings.'

'All right,' she shrugged, suddenly uncaring, 'apology accepted.'

'Vicky,' his eyes glinted with anger which took a moment to control, 'even you must see how easily I could make a mistake. Both you and Philip have been victims of your stepmother's callousness. I was only trying to help.'

'Your uncle, perhaps, but not me,' she pointed out coldly.

'What happened compelled me to seek revenge.'

'I was merely the innocent victim.'

As Vicky remained unimpressed, Nik's mouth tightened again. 'I intend making it up to you,' he snapped, looking faintly offended.

She gasped at him incredulously. As if he ever could! 'You're too kind,' she drawled deliberately.

He seemed uncertain of her in this mood and a frown marred his intelligent forehead. 'I've already got arrangements in hand,' he stated aloofly. 'You will no doubt regret your sharpness when you learn of my generosity, but first there are things I would like to know.'

So would she. What on earth he was talking about, for a start? Was he about to offer her a pension for life to make sure of getting rid of her? 'What is it you would like to know?' she asked bitterly.

'It might help if we began at the beginning,' he noted flatly. 'Why was the relationship between you and your stepmother so obviously bad?'

Vicky hadn't been expecting him to bother with that,

and her eyes were confused as she stared at the glass in her hand. 'Perhaps it wasn't anyone's fault,' she tried to be fair. 'Vera was only twenty-two when she married my father and I don't think she ever wanted a readymade family.'

'She never had one of her own?'

Vicky shook her head sadly. 'My father was much older.'

'No excuse,' Nik said curtly, then, 'She appears to have had a certain fondness for older men. Much older men.'

'Some women do.'

He ignored this contemptuously. 'So after your father died she threw you out.'

'Well, no,' Vicky stammered, 'I think my leaving was something we both decided on mutually.'

Nik's eyes narrowed with thoughtful suspicion. 'It couldn't have been your father's death which caused such a sudden decision?'

'I don't think I want to answer that.' Vicky's eyes blurred as she recalled the pain and agony she had suffered. She could never tell Nik the truth about Vera. It was better to remember and be grateful that she had escaped without being permanently scarred. 'Vera liked an entirely different way of life,' she hedged. 'It was better that we lived apart.'

'As you say,' he appeared willing to take her word for it. 'Now tell me, have you any idea why your stepmother should choose to assume your name when she came here?'

'No,' Vicky sighed defeatedly, 'I can only guess. She knew I worked for your firm, she probably checked from time to time that I was still there. She must have been staying on the island and heard of your uncle and decided it might be an easy way of introducing herself.'

'Wouldn't she have any fear of being found out?'

'She must have thought him wealthy enough to make the risk worthwhile.'

Nik stared at her contemplatively. 'Philip never worked in the family firm. My grandfather wanted him to, but he wasn't interested. He did quite well on his own, but he never made a fortune.'

'He appears to be well enough off.'

'Your stepmother must have had that impression too. His father left him some money and I help.'

'And when Vera discovered he wasn't a million-aire . . .' Vicky frowned.

'She extracted what she could and vanished,' Nik finished harshly.

Vicky knew she was very pale, she could feel it in the terrible coldness invading her cheeks. Vera had acted diabolically; someone should atone for her sins. There was little doubt in her mind that Vera would never do this herself. Knowing the whole situation, Vicky could understand Nik's determination to make someone suffer, yet she still found it difficult to forgive what he had done to her.

'And you decided to avenge your uncle,' she said coldly, the memory of his well thought out plans sticking in her throat.

Nik turned a grim face towards her. 'I went too far, I realise, on what was merely circumstantial evidence. Before I began it would have been easy enough to have proved who you were beyond doubt. That I believed I had is no excuse.'

He looked rather startled when she said, 'I quite agree,' and she wondered if anyone had ever been allowed to criticise him but himself. He was adept at the magnanimous gesture, but his generosity was rarely what it seemed. It was more often a trick to blind the eyes of its recipient to what was being concealed. He was astute and ruthless, and she didn't care to have these same traits aimed at her.

Quickly she grappled with pain, forcing herself to go on lightly. 'I was stupid too. You never said you loved me and several comments you made should have made

me suspicious sooner than I was that our engagement
was a sham.'

'I'm sorry, Vicky,' a faint red crept under the
tanned skin on his cheeks, 'I realise I've hurt you, but
I intend putting everything right. Before we return to
the U.K. we'll be married. I could scarcely do more
than that.'

A few weeks ago Vicky had longed to marry him;
now she froze. He talked as though he were conferring
a great honour; she was thankful she only felt inclined
to throw it back in his face. What would have happened
if she had been the lovelorn little fool of a few weeks
ago? She might have been kneeling at his feet thanking
him gratefully. Now she was able to look at him quite
indifferently and shrug, 'No, thank you!'

'You're insane!' The exclamation seemed torn from
him furiously, as if he had sustained a sharp shock. She
almost laughed at the way he controlled his visible fury
and decided to try a little charm.

His mouth eased in a gentle smile. 'I know you've
been under considerable stress, Vicky, so don't make
any hasty decisions. When you've had a rest and time to
think this over, you'll see it is the only thing to do.'

'Why?' she asked.

'Hell, Vicky,' he snapped, his impatience showing again,
ruffled by her deplorable coolness, 'it would be for your
sake as well as mine.'

'As well as yours!' She allowed her finely marked
brows to rise.

He noted their elevation with annoyance. 'Yes,' he
grated, 'I have a conscience to appease, haven't I?'

A conscience was the last thing she would credit him
with, she told herself bitterly. 'That's interesting,' she
retorted dryly.

She was amused by the outrage in his eyes until they
grew calculating. Then she knew it had been folly to
underestimate him. No one would be allowed to turn
down Nik Demetrious lightly. He had treated her

badly, but he would consider even his insult of a proposal more than adequate compensation.

'You haven't forgotten you love me?' he asked silkily, leaning nearer.

The triumph in his voice shook Vicky afresh. He had apologised, but never mentioned the weeks when his ill-treatment of her had made her nearly ill. She realised now the purpose behind his cruelty, but she hadn't then. Any caring man would have told her tenderly that he had been a brute and he was sorry, but not Nik! If she listened to him again, wouldn't she be laying herself open to the same kind of torture as soon as he tired of her? With women he was ruthless. The only time he showed sensitivity was when he was making love to them. His skill as a lover, she thought cynically, was something no one could doubt!

'You killed any love I had for you,' she said sharply, really believing she was speaking the truth.

'Love doesn't die so quickly,' he declared softly.

'If it isn't genuine in the first place, it doesn't have to die,' she retorted icily, hating his amused, mocking complacency. 'And if I did love you, I'd be a fool to marry you, knowing you didn't love me.'

'You never know what might come out of our marriage,' he said carefully, his thick lashes suddenly lowered so she couldn't read his expression.

'Is that a thought I'm supposed to cling to?' she cried tartly. 'What great comfort would that be?'

'Don't be stupid,' he snapped impatiently. 'It would surely mean something?'

'If I married you, which I certainly shan't!' she added hastily, 'what about poor Miss Becker?'

'Gilda?' There was genuine bewilderment in his eyes. 'You can forget about her. She doesn't mean a thing.'

His casual dismissal of the girl, accompanied by a careless smile, further incensed Vicky. She would have liked to have called him a conceited devil, but not even that, she suspected, would wipe the sharp amusement from his eyes.

'Were you very jealous of Gilda?' he asked under his breath.

She opened her mouth to protest, only to find his mouth descending to cover hers, smothering the retort coming hotly past her lips. For Vicky it was a case of mind over matter, a time for rigid control. Steadfastly she ignored the quick acceleration of her heart, the regrettable heat coursing through her body as Nik crushed her savagely in his arms. Whatever it was inside her that still urged her to respond to him, she mustn't give in to it. It was merely a physical obsession, which she had mistaken for love.

His lips forced hers apart with a seemingly passionate hunger when she would have closed them, and she ached from the deep, erotic movements of his hands against her skin. As his fingers curved possessively over her throbbing breast, the pressure of his mouth deepened and she shuddered as the force he used bent her head back until she feared her neck might break. Violently she wrenched away from him, landing him a stinging slap across his face.

Nik's hand came up savagely and grasped her neck. 'You little wildcat!' he gritted, his face livid as he caught her shoulders and shook her. 'I must be mad to offer marriage to such an ungrateful little bitch!'

'I refused,' she reminded him jerkily, as he thrust her from him and she tearfully touched her tender neck. 'That should have been the end of it.'

'Don't worry,' he snarled ferociously, his eyes glittering, 'I won't trouble you again. It's not as if I'm depriving myself. There are other women.'

'Only too willing,' she tacked on recklessly, shaking with reaction as the morning's events caught up with her in earnest. 'Tell me something I don't know!'

'When we return to London——' he began menacingly.

'I'll be leaving you,' she cut in tartly, trying to steady her trembling lips.

'Ah, but you won't!' he retorted suavely, grinning.

Startled, Vicky stared at him, remembering hearing the same words before. 'You can't intend holding me to our contract this time?' she asked incredulously.

'It still has several months to run,' he replied decisively.

'Nik!' Suddenly all the fight went out of her as she fought to keep back tears. 'Please let me go. I don't see how you can stop me, and even if you could, what would you gain by it.'

'A good secretary.' There was a sharp satisfaction in his voice she didn't like. 'What I said a couple of weeks ago still holds. I don't have to repeat it all, but I can add to it. You won't marry me, you say your love for me is dead, so what is there to bother you? Why should I deprive myself of your services, which I've already discovered are a cut above average, and I'm going to be too busy during the next few weeks to get used to another girl.'

'You could try!'

'How desperate you sound,' he smiled unsympathetically. 'There can't be anything you're afraid of now. The gossip will die down and you're due for a rise. And on top of that you'll earn extra, because there are a lot of functions I'm going to ask you to attend with me. If you're at all ambitious your future couldn't be rosier.'

What he said haunted Vicky for weeks afterwards. They stayed on Corfu another two days. She would have left immediately, but Nik insisted they must visit his aunt, as they had promised, and while he was on the island there was a lot to see to about the villa. Vicky couldn't dispute this, especially as Daphne told her he hadn't been here for a while, but all the time she was disturbed by his dark presence and fretting to be away.

Vicky was sure he enjoyed their stay more than she did, for he never missed an opportunity to snipe at her regarding her refusal to marry him. He had asked her to marry him and she supposed his conscience, on this score at least, must be clear, but his pride, at her refusal, had undoubtedly suffered a setback. He decided two days would give her a rest, but he certainly didn't give her much peace. Frequently, if coolly, he pointed out the position his wife would occupy; how he must soon begin looking around for a suitable woman to fill this position. Once when Vicky, feeling slightly ill, asked him if his Greek relations hadn't already chosen a bride for him, he had replied that there were one or two they had in mind who would be very happy to marry him.

They went to Athens before returning to London. On the morning they left Corfu she stood on the terrace overlooking the brilliant blue sea and wondered if she hadn't been crazy to turn Nik down, even if she no longer loved him. To be able to spend long weeks in places like this, soaking up the sun and peace, without having to worry over money, must be wonderful. Quickly she thrust such a temptation from her as Nik came to stand by her side. He wasn't for her, she firmly told the part of her that responded too swiftly to his dark masculinity. He could undoubtedly supply all the comfort and luxury anyone might need but she was wise enough to know that nothing could compensate for a lack of affection.

'When I was here in the spring,' she tried carefully to keep off the very personal topics both her own thoughts and Nik had baited her with during the past forty-eight hours, 'there were flowers everywhere.' She remembered the waves of colour over the hillsides. All the English flowers had been there; the daisies, buttercups, dandelions, clovers, herbs and vetch, but many, many more. She recalled the sheets of shimmering blue campanula covering the roadside verges, the giant fennel, wild orchids and others too numerous to mention.

Nik glanced at her broodingly a few moments before

replying. 'The flowers come twice a year. During the long summer drought most of them die, but in the autumn, after the rain, they get another chance, unlike some human beings.'

Was he talking of her or himself, or perhaps just generally? While she was trying to decide from the note in his voice, the helicopter that was to take them to Athens arrived.

'Here we go,' Nik murmured, shading his eyes to watch the machine land against the glare of the sun. Abruptly he asked, 'Are you glad we came?'

His query took her by surprise and she replied without thinking. 'If it means the end of your suspicion and hate, yes. Otherwise I don't see how we could possibly have gone on working together.'

His mouth curled. 'A girl who can turn her back so easily on the good things of life should surely find no hardship in coping with its difficulties.'

Vicky clenched her hands. 'No one likes constant irritation.'

'Was that all I was?'

Damn him, Vicky thought. She would give him full marks for being unreasonable! He twisted everything she said, turning it to his own advantage. She was relieved when the helicopter pilot jumped to the ground and approached them, enabling her to avoid answering Nik's cutting question. He didn't persist, but all the way to Athens she sensed he was angry.

If Vicky's nerves had been raw on Corfu, a week in Athens did nothing to improve them. As in New York, Nik refused to let her near the office where he worked, or to carry out any duties as his secretary. He said Miss Devlin would look after him again, and that it might be wiser for Vicky to keep out of her way. Miss Devlin, he'd added, Vicky thought cunningly, knew of their broken engagement, and he didn't want to expose Vicky to either her sympathy or curiosity.

While refusing to believe he could be so concerned

for her, Vicky forbore to comment. Nor did she say anything when he told her she could amuse herself in the apartment while he was busy. If she wanted to go out she must take one of the manservants with her. On no account should she go out alone.

Vicky would rather have used the metro than the chauffeur-driven car he provided. Usually she chose to walk, and even with the restrictive presence of a burly manservant by her side she managed to see quite a lot of the city. She would certainly have enjoyed herself if she had been on a proper holiday, but the knowledge that she must return and face Nik each evening became increasingly unbearable. The tension between them seemed to be getting worse instead of better. Sometimes, inexplicably, she felt it was so taut it must snap, and she dared not speculate on the consequences. It disconcerted her that her heart still tripped unsteadily when he looked at her intently and that his nearness could still do insane things to her senses. Yet when she hinted, pointedly, that it might be easier if they spent their evenings apart, he appeared completely indifferent to her feelings.

She had never seen the blood run so fast to his face as it did when she said that. He had turned swiftly, on a muttered curse and walked from the room, but the set of his broad shoulders had marked his cold rage.

'I don't care for my staff telling me what to do—or what not to do!' he had snapped harshly, half turning in the doorway.

Most evenings when he arrived home, he went straight to the shower. Then he usually came to find Vicky, insolently wearing a short bath robe or sometimes only a thick towel tied round his middle.

He didn't seem to notice the strain this put on her as she tried to look anywhere but at his semi-nakedness while he told her where they would be dining that evening. Occasionally they stayed in the apartment, but more often he took her out to some good hotel or inn. On their last evening, in a famous casino outside the city, he laughed when she lost all the money he had forcibly thrust in her handbag.

The disappointment on her face must have been slightly ludicrous, but his laughter grated and her eyes flashed with anger.

'Don't look so annoyed,' he grinned, lifting her chin so her eyes met his.

'How can you tell I'm annoyed?' She jerked her head away sharply.

'You're as transparent as glass,' he said. 'At least you used to be,' he muttered more curtly.

Vicky flushed, wanting to hit him. Need he remind her of all the times she had told him she loved him, of how she had gazed at him in undisguised adoration?

'Did you hope to make a fortune and become completely independent?' he mocked as they left.

'It doesn't take a fortune!' she snapped.

'You can't be independent while you're tied to me,' he retorted, his mouth hard as he hustled her into his car.

She didn't like his phraseology. It smacked of a truth she wasn't prepared to admit. 'In a few months' time I will be,' she muttered fiercely, taking pleasure in seeing his own anger rise.

It was their last night. Tomorrow they were returning to London. Vicky didn't know if she was actually looking forward to this. She had been glad enough to escape the speculation in numerous faces, but she didn't suppose, despite Nik's assurances, that anything would have changed during the short time they had been away. She realised very few people would have shown any interest if she had been engaged to someone ordinary. That was the price she had to pay for getting involved with Nik Demetrious.

In the apartment she said goodnight without lingering, merely shaking her head when Nik suggested a drink. Quickly she closed the door of her bedroom, leaning against it for a moment, trying not to tremble. She hated him, didn't she, so why did she allow him so easily to get under her skin? Perhaps it would be better in London? With the whole upsetting business of Nik's uncle and Vera behind her, she would be able to begin again. Gordon had, in the past, often asked her to go out with him, but she had always refused. She wouldn't, she vowed, if he asked her again. She might have to work for Nik but, socially anyway, she wouldn't be seeing anything of him after this.

Putting a hand to the zipper of her dress, she cursed to find it was stuck. For quite ten minutes she wrestled with it before giving up. Nik might still be in the lounge, although she hesitated to approach him. Then she chided herself for being so silly. He hadn't touched her since they had left Corfu; it was highly unlikely that he would do so now! If he did, all she need do was tell him to get lost!

She didn't find him either in the lounge or his study, where one of the servants had told her he often worked until dawn. Wearily Vicky decided she would sleep in her dress and ask the maid who brought her morning tea to unzip her. It mightn't be very comfortable, but there was no point in rousing anyone now.

She had to pass Nik's bedroom door to reach her own, and she was startled when it opened.

'Can't you sleep?' she heard him asking mockingly.

She spun round, shockingly shaken. 'What a fright you gave me!'

'It was mutual,' he replied dryly. 'I heard someone prowling around and I thought everyone was in bed.'

He didn't look equipped to deal with a burglar, if one had possibly managed to penetrate this far, unless it was with his bare fists. He was wearing pants and nothing else, having obviously been getting ready for bed, and the strength of his arms, thus revealed, made Vicky shudder for the fate of any intruder.

'I—I was having trouble with my zip,' she stammered.
'I thought you might still be up.'

'Ah, a cry for help?' he drawled. 'So what were you
going to do when I wasn't there?'

'Sleep in my dress,' she said tensely.

'Turn round,' he commanded, his grey eyes glinting
through half-closed lids.

He fumbled so long she could have screamed. His
fingers were usually so nimble she wouldn't have
thought it would have taken him more than seconds.

'I can't see properly,' he said at last. 'Some of the
material is caught. We'll have to go to your room where
the light is better.'

She blinked uncertainly at the dim light above her
head, feeling in no position to argue. Perhaps it was?
'Come on then,' she shrugged, leading the way.

CHAPTER EIGHT

Zips caught in material are a modern hazard. It had happened to Vicky before. 'Try easing it gently up and down,' she suggested anxiously. Did Nik have to close the door?

'I've got it!' he exclaimed triumphantly, and she made a wild grab at her dress as he released her from it and it fell to the floor.

As she bent to pick it up he grasped her hands. 'Leave it,' he said thickly, his glance smouldering over her scantily clad curves.

Blushing, Vicky struggled to free herself. 'Let go of me!' she cried, stepping back too hastily and falling in an ignominious heap as she tripped over the dress draped round her ankles.

Nik fell with her, right on top of her and with her feet still caught she couldn't break free of him. His growling laughter in her ears made her even more furious. What right had he to laugh at her, damn him? He had been laughing at her all evening, and she didn't enjoy his perverted kind of humour.

Neither did she enjoy it when he suddenly stopped laughing and began kissing her, deep, drugging kisses that robbed her of her remaining breath. She caught the silvery glitter of his eyes for a moment before his mouth forced her head back, parting her lips hungrily as if he had been waiting for this for days.

Blood rushed to her face and every other part of her. She could feel herself shaking, despite the rigid control she put on herself. She could feel a traitorous weakness flooding her limbs and knew she had to do something before it was too late. Fiercely she fought to lever herself out from under him, which wasn't easy when she scarcely knew what she was doing.

He freed her hands to find the catch on her bra and with a horrified gasp she heard the fastener snap and his finger began rubbing a distended nipple. 'Stop it!' she whispered in a strangled voice, trying to push him away.

Her frantic efforts were ineffective. He took no notice as he took his mouth from hers and lowered it to her breast. 'For heaven's sake, Vicky,' he groaned as she stiffened convulsively, 'if you won't marry me at least let me love you.'

'No!' Vicky was aware of the danger she was in as his excitement showed through his roughening breath. He gripped her tightly while his lips trailed a passionate path over her bare skin. His body lay heavily against her, his heart making direct contact with her pounding one, their simultaneous beat threatening to deprive her of her last remaining senses.

'Vicky!' he entreated hoarsely, 'do you want to drive me out of my mind?'

If he hadn't spoken she might have given in to him. She had been beginning to forget everything, yielding mindlessly to the strange, burning ache inside her. A realisation of what she was doing combined with panic and fear to give her sufficient strength to hit out at him. 'No!' she cried wildly, pushing at the wide shoulders, with a shocked pang suddenly aware that they were both practically naked.

'Shush,' he muttered thickly, crushing her mouth to silence with hot, devouring kisses. 'Be still!'

Vicky shuddered as she tried to fight being dominated by the hard, sensual face above her. It shocked her, as greatly as it had done on Corfu, that physically she should still be attracted to him. 'If you don't let go of me, you great brute, I'll scream!' she promised raggedly as momentarily Nik raised himself to stare down at her.

His eyes bored into her mutinous ones as his lips

parted in an angry sneer. 'You don't have one original thought in your head, do you? Who's going to hear?'

'How else can I fight you?' she gasped.

'I could take you.' He was smiling and she hated the confidence in his voice. 'No man has yet, have they, Vicky?'

She wished he had put out the light so he wouldn't have seen her humiliating blush. She didn't need to answer.

'Don't tell me I'm the only man who has ever desired you?'

'You might lose interest if I said yes.'

'I've seen other men looking at you. I can read their minds.' They were talking in unnatural whispers. Nik sounded hoarse, his face oddly flushed as his eyes roamed restlessly over her slim, seductive body, her huge violet eyes and wide, soft mouth. Usually she looked fragile and pale, but now there was a wild colour under her skin which held his attention.

'You aren't as indifferent to me as you think you are,' he rasped.

'I'm working on it,' she retorted, feeling sick. She noticed the corded veins on his neck standing out as his mouth came towards her again and knew he intended making her eat her words. She felt the crush of his body reimposing itself and had to clench her teeth against his marauding lips. With all her strength she tore herself out of his arms.

'One day you won't say no,' he snarled, leaping to his feet, 'if I ever give you another chance?'

How was it, Vicky wondered dully, that no matter what the situation, he never looked anything but magnificent? Rejection only made him look grimly arrogant, increasing his attraction, which was evidenced by the peculiar little shiver that ran through her. Blindly she stared at his powerful features, the hard, sensual mouth, trying fiercely to concentrate on all that was bad in him.

'It's not long since you couldn't try hard enough to get rid of me!' she retorted, grabbing her robe from the bed and struggling into it with her back to him.

He made no attempt to help her. 'You've got your arm through the wrong sleeve,' he taunted. 'But you don't have to put it on. I'm going.'

'Good!' she snapped.

'Keep on as you're doing, Miss Brown, and no man's going to be interested in what you're trying to cover up!'

As the door slammed, Vicky thought she must need her head examined ever to have imagined she loved anyone as insensitive and callous. Her cheeks burned with an embarrassment she tried to get rid of under a cold shower, but she felt little better when later she crawled into bed. Would she ever be immune to what he did, she wondered, with a touch of desperation, or indifferent to the things he said? When no immediate answer was forthcoming, with a muffled sob she pulled the satin sheets over her head.

In London, she had told herself, she would soon be free at least of his disturbing presence, but in thinking this she made another mistake. It was late evening when they returned and Nik insisted she spent the night at his apartment, rather than go back to an empty house.

'I won't allow it,' he said curtly. 'It's after ten and you've been gone almost two weeks. For a start, you won't have any food in.'

'I could borrow from my neighbour,' she glared at him stubbornly.

'Don't argue, child,' he replied, just as adamantly.

Later, in yet another of his satin-sheeted beds, Vicky fumed helplessly. Yet, as she relaxed, the trend of her thoughts changed. She wondered at the subtle shift in their relationship. Nik was again the domineering boss, but there was a new familiarity in his manner which hadn't been there before. It was almost proprietorial, and she wondered how it had evolved out of the debris of their broken engagement. They should have been strangers, but in some strange, incomprehensible way they seemed closer than they had ever been.

Nik woke her the following morning to tell her they were going straight in to work. When she protested that she had nothing to wear, he raised a bored brow and said she had the clothes she had worn in Greece. Feeling that one of her now rather creased cottons was anything but suitable for a chairman's secretary, she dressed hastily and had only time for a quick cup of coffee before leaving with him for the office.

As they entered the huge, modern vestibule, the attention of numerous members of his staff became riveted on them. Mostly there were murmurs of— 'Good morning, sir. Nice to have you back again, sir.' Vicky was ignored. Bowing and scraping wasn't in it! she thought, with an almost audible little sniff which, on second thoughts, she hoped Nik didn't hear.

He might have done, for his eyes suddenly narrowed. He was walking closely beside her, not holding her arm but keeping his own too near for her liking. When she tried to put some distance between them, he closed ranks and proceeded to make several low-toned remarks.

Vicky frowned as she saw one or two eyebrows lifting and resolved not to arrive with him again. She envied Nik his indifference, but he surely wasn't so insensible that he didn't realise the close attention which, for some reason, he was deliberately paying her might result in making tongues wag again?

She was so relieved to see Gordon, she almost threw her arms round him. If Nik hadn't been there she might have done. As it was she contented herself with giving him a glowing smile.

'Hello, Vicky darling,' he beamed, 'it's good to see you.'

'It's lovely to see you,' she laughed. 'And I remembered to buy you a present.'

'Ooh, a present!' he exclaimed in delight, teasingly. 'What is it? I can't wait!'

'If you two have quite finished!' Nik cut in sharply. 'I don't pay people to stand around.'

Gordon, familiar with his moods, didn't take offence, he merely apologised lightly.

Nik nodded. 'Perhaps we can get on. Has Henderson heard anything more about the *Attika* from Lloyds since yesterday, do you know? And Veiga. What's the position there?'

Gordon said yes to his first query and, much the same, to his second, and hastened to his office for the relevant details, while Nik disappeared into his and Vicky began sorting her desk. The way Nik kept track of everything that went on amazed her. He never missed a thing. Veiga, she knew, ran cruise ships. They were a small concern but surprisingly successful. Nik had some shares, but there was a rumour, which was something more than just a rumour, that the chairman was retiring, and Nik had been on to it for weeks.

Gordon told her more about it over lunch. This was the first time she had lunched with him, but she had felt strangely depressed all morning and had been glad to accept his invitation. While they were drinking their coffee she gave him the amusing piece of Greek art she had picked up in Athens and he mentioned Veiga.

'Do you think he'll sell out to Nik?' she asked.

'Shush!' Gordon laughed. 'Keep your voice down. No one's supposed to know Nik's interested.'

She smiled. 'So what happens next?'

'Veiga's a wily old bird,' Gordon grinned. 'He wants to sell out, but he'd like to keep it in the family.'

'How's he going to do that?'

Gordon shrugged wryly. 'You may well ask, but it's not all that difficult to see the way his mind's working. He has an unmarried daughter and Nik hasn't a wife. Oh, I'm sorry, Vicky,' he stammered, his face bright red with embarrassment, 'I wasn't thinking.'

'That's all right, Gordon,' Vicky forgave him, 'I'm over it now. I think the trip to Greece did the trick.'

His face brightened, as this news tallied with secret ambitions of his own. He looked at her almost eagerly. 'That's the best bit of news I've heard in a long time!'

Vicky hoped he didn't make too much of it, although she tried to smile back convincingly. She rubbed her face with a thoughtful forefinger, wondering why it felt so stiff. Slowly she said, 'Does Mr Veiga have a hope of tempting Nik that way? He doesn't have to marry money, does he?'

Gordon's shoulders lifted and dropped. 'No, I guess not, but Miss Veiga is rumoured to be beautiful, and if her old man's little lot comes with her—well, who can resist a bargain?'

They returned to the office five minutes early, so that couldn't be the reason Nik glared at her. It was unusual to find he hadn't gone out for his own lunch but had apparently had something sent in to him.

Vicky eyed the wilting sandwiches doubtfully. 'I'm sorry, I didn't realise you intended staying in.'

'Another time make sure, won't you?' His voice was expressionless but somehow made her feel he might have died with starvation. 'That fool girl in there,' he was obviously referring to Vicky's assistant, 'ordered something revolting!'

The sandwiches, when fresh, were very nice. Vicky had them herself frequently and he must know that. She decided not to feel too sorry for him. 'Gordon shouldn't be a minute,' she smiled, thinking Nik must be waiting for him. 'He got waylaid on the way up.'

'You've been lunching together?'

'Yes,' she heaved a rueful sight. 'We had a lovely lunch, but I think I ate too much. It was kind of him, though, and I won't need much dinner.'

'Hasn't he asked you out for that as well? Obviously he's hoping to catch you on the rebound.'

At last Nik's contemptuous tones got through to her.

Vicky drew a sharp breath, returning glare for glare. Miss Veiga was welcome to him! Not that she had much hope of getting him. Nik was too used to playing the field to be so easily caught, even if the trap was attractively baited.

She felt herself going curiously cold as her eyes dropped and she turned from him.

'Oh, by the way,' his voice halted her, 'there's a party I want you to attend with me tomorrow evening.'

He might have struck her with less effect. Her blue eyes widened as she swung back to him. 'But we're not engaged any more.'

'Just as well.' He sat down with satisfaction.

What kind of answer was that? She tried not to think of the obvious one. Angrily she stammered, 'S-some people might think it strange if we still go about together.'

'Is there something wrong with your memory, Miss Brown? Didn't I mention,' he snapped, 'I would require you to accompany me to various functions?'

Her heart began beating with heavy strokes of suspicion. 'You did, but I didn't take you seriously.'

'Remarkable,' he jeered.

She shivered, recognising he was in a foul temper and wishing Gordon would hurry up. 'I realise there are occasions when you need a secretary, but I didn't know these included parties. Who's giving this one?' she asked carefully, fearing she already knew the answer.

'Someone called Veiga. You must have heard of him?'

Vicky merely nodded, she didn't say how recently. 'I'll look forward to it,' she lied.

'Don't overdo the enthusiasm, Miss Brown.'

Sarcastic beast! She wondered if the squeamishness in her stomach had to do with the way his eyes went insolently over her, or if it was something she had eaten. Ignoring what he said, she hurriedly excused herself, and this time he didn't try and stop her.

That night she dreamt Nik was swimming in deep waters and Veiga was dangling his daughter from the end of a hook—a beautiful fly Nik swallowed willingly. When Vicky woke with a start, the dream was still with her vividly. It would serve him right if it really happened, she thought morosely, trying to envisage him stretched out helplessly on the shore with Veiga and his daughter gloating triumphantly over him.

Restlessly Vicky punched her pillow. Why didn't such a picture appeal to her? Her throat hurt as though she was the one who had actually swallowed the hook. Nik wasn't as helpless as all that, she reminded herself. In fact he wasn't helpless at all, he had his moves all planned out, which was why he was taking her with him to this party. Vicky thought she could read his mind like a book! If Miss Veiga didn't suit him, he had her to fall back on. People knew she was his secretary and might also know she had been his fiancée. Deviously he was using their broken engagement to suit his own ends because having Vicky clamped to his side would provide just sufficient mystery to keep everyone guessing. If Miss Veiga suited his purpose and he found her agreeable, Vicky had little doubt she would soon be told to get lost!

The following afternoon, while arranging when to pick her up, Nik told her to wear something suitable. By that she imagined he meant something capable of making her fade into the background. The white dress she eventually chose seemed the very thing. She didn't notice that although the colour was certainly un-obtrusive, the cut of it was not. With her fair hair brushed thick and gleaming over her slender shoulders and her soft, full mouth touched with a lovely shade of pink, it made her look sexy yet completely young and innocent at the same time.

She had bought the dress on impulse, in Athens, and had never had it on. It was only as she gazed doubtfully at her reflection before leaving that some of its impact began getting through to her, but Nik's arrival precluded any chance of changing it. With a resigned shrug she threw her velvet cloak swiftly around her shoulders and went to let him in.

She was still struggling with a strand of trapped hair as she opened the door and she didn't see how his mouth tightened as he stared at her. The dark blue velvet of the cloak exactly matched her eyes, while the chain which fastened it at her neck, in which, unfortunately, her hair had caught, gave her an enchanting, medieval look.

'Sorry,' she said breathlessly, her hair freed at last but her lashes fluttering as she tried not to out-stare him. He was so handsome in his superbly cut evening attire that she could scarcely drag her eyes away from his tall, erect figure.

'No need to apologise, I'm three minutes early,' he said brusquely, barely glancing at her again as she walked down the steps beside him and got into his car. Dion was driving. Nik tucked in a corner of Vicky's cloak and slid in the back beside her. He remained silent and a little grim.

Vicky couldn't help shooting anxious glances at his chiselled profile, wondering why he was so stern. She lived in Bloomsbury and was vaguely aware of the car travelling smoothly along Boswell Street, into Southampton Row, then Kingsway, towards the Strand and the Embankment and the entrance of the Savoy Hotel.

'Mr Veiga is certainly doing things in style!' she said sharply, tense from Nik's prolonged silence.

'You'll enjoy it,' he replied crisply, 'and it won't do you any harm. You need more self-confidence.'

'Not everyone's used to such places,' she said defensively, 'But I'm not exactly shaking in my shoes.'

'Just stick by me,' he advised coldly, 'and you'll be all right.'

Would she? Vicky grew more doubtful by the minute

as they entered the reception area of the suite where the party was being held. She wasn't frightened of the people so much as the glitter, and even this, though everyone looked as if they owned at least a million dollars, wasn't the real cause of her despair. The real cause of her despondency was something she didn't want to think about.

The room they passed into was huge and equally crowded with sophisticated guests. Drink was flowing like the Thames outside and a small, select band was playing in one corner. Vicky was conscious of many pairs of eyes swivelling to glance at Nik as they came in. His reputation as a wealthy business man was well known, as were his tough, distinctive features, and he moved with an assurance which spoke for itself. Vicky was glad of her elegant dress, although she realised it wasn't she who was attracting the attention.

Nik was hailed from all sides, and it amazed her the skill he displayed in avoiding most who tried to speak to him. He did it so charmingly no one took offence, while all the time he kept his hand under Vicky's arm, refusing to let her go even when she twisted discreetly in an effort to get away from him.

'Behave yourself!' he hissed in her ear, his breath actually stirring her hair.

Hating him for the obvious speculation this aroused, she gave in, though all her senses advised her not to. She was possessed by an urgent desire to meet Mr Veiga and his daughter, to see for herself if Miss Veiga was beautiful, but she shrank from the disturbance such a meeting might inflict. She had no idea how she would react to seeing Nik with another woman, and she had no particular wish to find out.

Someone tapped her on the arm. It was Sir Clive Martin. 'Hello, darling,' he smiled, looking very pleased with himself.

Nik said coldly but pointedly, 'Nice to see you, Clive. How is your wife?'

Clive shrugged and asked Vicky to dance. He smiled into her eyes and glanced at her ringless fingers. 'Perhaps I should ask how is your engagement? I believe you two have decided you weren't meant for each other after all?'

Nik ignored this, although his face stiffened. 'Vicky can dance with you later. I'm going to get her a drink, if you'll excuse us.'

As Nik dragged her away, she stared at him indignantly. 'How do you know I don't want to dance now?'

'Anything to oblige,' he murmured suavely, sweeping her on to the dance-floor. 'I thought you would be too thirsty to be thinking of immediate exercise. After this kindly make your wishes clearer.'

He was impossible! Vicky felt so angry she almost tripped and could have slapped the satisfied grin from his face as this forced her to cling to him briefly while she regained her balance.

'It's your dress,' as she glared at him, his eyes blatantly gazed down on her half exposed breasts. 'Such deplorable taste asks for everything it gets.'

'What's wrong with it this time?' She remembered how he had criticised the one she had worn to meet his uncle on Corfu and her lips pursed mutinously.

'You're coming out of it, for one thing,' he snapped.

'Of course I'm not!' she protested. 'If you take a look round at the other women's dresses, you'll see that mine's quite modest by comparison.'

'Not many of the other women have as much to show as you have,' he said insolently.

Colour surged under Vicky's skin, a wild pink toning incredibly with her mouth, briefly changing the direction of his attention. It was the kind of personal remark she never associated with him, the kind he appeared to keep exclusively for her! As steadily as she was able, she said, 'I'm sure you exaggerate, and I'll wear what I choose, just as I also claim the right to choose my own friends.'

'Well just bear in mind that Clive Martin is married,'
he said coldly. 'His title might be irresistible, but he also
has a jealous wife.'

'And I have an unreasonable employer!' she retorted
furiously.

'If we were alone I could answer that more
effectively,' he snapped, his tightening arms reflecting
his thoughts so excruciatingly that she gasped.

Feeling impinged against every hard bone of his
body, Vicky shivered in the steel strength of his
embrace. Her heart was racing and Nik moved his
thumb knowingly to the pulse in her wrist. She began
shaking hard and was so terrified that she stiffened and
pulled away from him.

With no clear answer in her head as to why she was
so frequently doing this, she was dismayed to find
herself bumping clumsily into a man approaching them.
He apologised, charmingly taking the blame, but
instead of passing on he spoke to Nik.

'I'm sorry I missed you when you arrived, Mr
Demetrious. I was unavoidably detained.'

Nik, coming up behind Vicky, smiled and shook
hands. 'I've been dancing with my secretary,' formally
he introduced her, 'Miss Brown, Mr Veiga.'

'Good, good!' Veiga might easily have rubbed his
hands together. 'I hoped you wouldn't—er—get
involved with anyone before you met my daughter.'

Vicky was infuriated that they talked as if she didn't
exist. Nik had passed her off as of no account, while Mr
Veiga obviously looked on her as such, from the way he
had worded his sentence. Of course, that was all she
was, a piece of office equipment. From her presence
Veiga would merely deduce that Nik meant business.

'Ah, your daughter!'

She heard Nik speaking with warm anticipation and
winced at such a note in his voice. Mr Veiga nodded
happily and said, 'Come with me, she's over here.'

Vicky was again conscious of Nik's hold on her arm

as they followed Mr Veiga and kept her unhappy gaze
fixed on the back of Mr Veiga's head. Like Nik, he had
a faintly foreign accent, and while he was older she
sensed, in his own way, that he might be just as devious.
They would make formidable apponents, but Nik, she
suspected ironically, might just have the edge.

Rita Veiga was a girl in her middle twenties and very
beautiful. She was tall and statuesque, her short, dark
hair sculptured around her proud head, emphasising a
dazzling white complexion and ruby-red lips. Her eyes
were large and bold, her figure voluptuous. Vicky felt
dwarfed by her in every way.

Nik looked impressed. Vicky frowned as he stared at
Miss Veiga intently, unable to believe his surrender
could be as complete as it looked. He asked her to
dance as though he couldn't wait to get her to himself
and seemed to forget all about Vicky or Miss Veiga's
father. Placing a hand on her waist, he whirled her
away without ever taking his eyes off her.

Vicky was aware of a consuming sickness rising in
her throat as she briefly lowered her thick lashes to hide
the sight of them. Mr Veiga, by her side, purred like a
tomcat having someone stroking his fur. He, too, was
watching the other couple, but his expression was vastly
different from Vicky's.

'A handsome couple, Miss Brown, don't you think?'

Vicky was trying not to. 'Yes,' she murmured,
swallowing.

He must have noticed she was pale and stopped a
waiter to get her a Martini. When she gave him a
grateful smile he obviously took it as a good sign, for he
grinned conspiringly. 'We'll save the champagne for
later, eh, Miss Brown?'

He was drinking vodka and as the waiter replenished
his glass he glanced at her innocently. 'There's a
rumour that Mr Demetrious was recently betrothed?'

'He was . . .'

'But not now?'

'No, it's all over.' Vicky gulped her Martini and had another immediately placed in her hand. If she suspected Mr Veiga of deliberately trying to loosen her tongue, she suddenly didn't care.

Smiling blandly, Mr Veiga remarked, 'As you are his secretary, I can rely on you to know the truth on such matters. Otherwise one doesn't know what to believe.'

Vicky hoped her face didn't look as hot as it felt. He obviously had no idea it was she who had been Nik's fiancée, and she saw no reason to tell him. She couldn't bear to see the curiosity which would surely dawn in his eyes if she did, neither did she feel like answering any more questions. Idly shrugging her delicate shoulders, she merely nodded.

Mr Veiga nodded as well, clearly very excited and determined to make the most of such an unexpected opportunity. She could almost see his brain ticking over—he might never get Nik's secretary alone again! 'Mr Demetrious doesn't usually spend so much time in London?'

'Unless there's a special reason.' She frowned, only just realising how true this was. Until she started working as his secretary she had scarcely thought about him, but she had known he was rarely there. If she hadn't seen him there had always been enough talk about him. The mistake he had made over his uncle must account for the weeks he had spent in London recently, but that couldn't be why he stayed on now.

Mr Veiga said quietly, 'When he prefers working in New York or Athens, do you think it's interest in my retirement which is keeping him here, Miss Brown?'

Vicky felt a stir of surprise. This was news indeed! Straight from the horse's mouth! Wouldn't Gordon have given an eye-tooth to have heard it first! But why was Mr Veiga talking to her?

She was soon to learn. Mr Veiga backpedalled, but not much. 'I would like to retire, Miss Brown, but not until my daughter's future is settled.'

At last Vicky thought she understood. She was expected to convey this discreetly back to Nik, a word in his ear. Veiga must be delighted she was here!

'My daughter is such a high-spirited girl. She needs a firm hand,' Mr Veiga sighed on, 'and when I retire I would like to live in Brazil, while Rita prefers other places.'

'Couldn't she live on her own?'

He sighed again. 'I am most reluctant to leave a young girl of her innocence alone in a large city.'

Innocence? Vicky had a struggle to keep a dry note from her voice. 'I understand,' she murmured.

'I knew you would,' he smiled warmly. 'I hoped I could count on your sympathy, my dear, and I assure you it won't go unrewarded.'

Getting his message clearer by the minute, Vicky was secretly appalled, but she didn't know how to shut him up. Didn't he realise she instinctively disliked his daughter and that, as Nik's secretary, she was in an extremely difficult position? If she did anything but nod and agree, she was sure Nik might easily murder her. When Clive Martin came up and asked her to dance again she accepted gratefully and tried not to think of Nik's wrath or Mr Veiga's hurt expression.

'Did I interrupt something?' Clive asked, smelling a mystery.

Coolly Vicky shook her head.

'I'm dying to hear what happened to your engagement,' he smiled at her persuasively as they joined the throng on the floor.

'We made a mistake,' Vicky replied stiffly, wondering if, in leaving Mr Veiga, she hadn't jumped straight from the frying-pan into the fire.

'I could have told you that, darling.' Clive's eyes devoured her no less enthusiastically than they had done when they first met. 'Nik's a fool, all the same. He seems to be taking a great interest in Rita Veiga.'

'I know nothing about that,' Vicky declared woodenly.

'Don't you?' he murmured silkily. 'Miss Veiga is a very wealthy young woman.'

While hating his sly insinuations against Nik, Vicky had no intention of sticking up for him. Even so, she was relieved to catch a glimpse of Nik approaching, although she wasn't prepared to find herself whipped as suddenly from Clive's arms.

'Excuse me,' Nik cut in curtly.

Clive protested in a peeved voice, 'Is it absolutely necessary?'

Nik glared at him without replying, taking Vicky away.

'You could have let us finish,' she said bitterly.

'Didn't I tell you to stay with Veiga?'

He had done no such thing! He hadn't mentioned the man's name other than that it was his reception they were attending. 'Any special reason why?' she asked coldly.

He shot her a sharp glance. 'I'm willing to bet you know, but it's not something I'm spreading around.'

'You mean you fancy his daughter?' She deliberately misunderstood.

His eyes smouldered. 'What if I do? At least it would stop me thinking of you.'

'Ah, the guilty conscience!' she retorted maliciously. 'It's not something to be alone with.'

'My problems aren't anything to what yours will be if you continue encouraging Clive Martin,' he snapped.

'I wasn't encouraging him!' she blazed, adding bleakly, 'Do you really believe I would want to be involved with another man so soon after you?'

'I hurt you that much?' Nik's dark face looked suddenly eager, the light hand he had placed on her waist digging into her.

'I'm over it now,' she flushed angrily at what she took to be amusement in his eyes. 'You can stop worrying.'

That didn't seem to please him, but they had halted

beside their host and he didn't get a chance to reply. Vicky smiled at Mr Veiga and his daughter brightly. It seemed easier to smile when Nik was scowling at them.

Mr Veiga threw her a slightly reproachful glance, but looked relieved that Nik was back. Then he ordered champagne, and she panicked. Did they have something to celebrate already? Had she missed something? She couldn't bear to wait and see.

'I—I have a dreadful headache,' she said to Nik. 'Would you mind if I went home?'

'If you must,' he frowned.

Vicky could see he was trying to judge if she was telling the truth, but that he didn't appear over-reluctant to let her go made her regret her hasty decision. He might even be pleased to get rid of her. She noticed how Miss Veiga slid her hands through his arm and hung on to him. Nik had obviously decided Rita was very much to his liking and would be pleased to feel free to concentrate on her for the rest of the evening.

'While you're collecting your cloak I'll get hold of Dion,' he said, 'and see you to the car.'

CHAPTER NINE

VICKY was scarcely in the office next morning before Nik rang.

'Send Miss Veiga some flowers,' he commanded, with what she considered a stupid smile on his face. 'She's a charming girl, as well as a very beautiful one.'

Vicky, feeling neither charming or beautiful after a restless night, said flatly, 'You appear to like her.'

'Any reason why I shouldn't?'

'Plenty why you should!' Vicky turned the pages of her pad unnecessarily.

'Explain yourself, Miss Brown!'

The Miss Browns were getting more frequent! Miserably she bowed her head, startled to find herself on the verge of tears. It must be the sharpness of his voice when she wasn't ready for it? 'Mr Veiga did hint he might be selling out.'

'So you think, or you gathered, that his daughter is part of the deal?'

She could feel his eyes boring into her and glanced up mutinously. 'Wouldn't Miss Veiga be the most attractive thing about it?'

'If one was interested?' he replied remotely.

Did he mean in Veiga's ships or his daughter? Why didn't he explain himself better? She tried to say that both might be his for the asking but somehow the words stuck in her throat. Let him find out for himself, she thought, if he hadn't already.

'How much longer are you going to stand there daydreaming?' she heard Nik ask bitingly, when she made no comment.

'I'm waiting for you to tell me what kind of flowers you want,' she said sharply. 'Forget-me-nots?'

'Just get on with it, won't you,' he muttered contemptuously. 'I'm in no mood this morning to appreciate your particular kind of wit.'

In her own office, Vicky ordered the most expensive flowers the florist had, then buried her face in her hands, briefly letting the unhappiness of the last weeks flood over her in waves. Who was she fooling in believing she was cured of the love she felt for Nik? Hearing her assistant arriving with Gordon, she took several deep breaths, regaining her composure just as they walked in. She noticed how well they got on together, these two, and a trace of envy touched her. Gordon didn't realise yet that he was attracted to Jenny, but one day he would. Perhaps, Vicky sighed, if Nik and she had been able to build up their relationship from the foundations of an ordinary friendship their romance might have stood a better chance.

Nik was short with her all morning. This wasn't the first time she had known his anger and she struggled desperately not to let it get under her skin. Gordon took it with a shrug, but Nik flicked her on the raw so often that by one she felt a mass of invisible bruises.

Then, to her stunned surprise, he asked her to have lunch with him. Gordon had left for his after casting her a wryly sympathetic glance. From the amount of work Nik piled on her he had naturally surmised she would be staying in.

This was what Vicky had intended. And she had no wish to lunch with Nik. She feared he might want to know in detail everything Mr Veiga had said at the party. Nik's mind was like a computer; he digested information and stored it—small scraps of no immediate consequence but which frequently helped him, at some later date, to come up with the right answers. He would want to squeeze her mind of information while it was still fresh, but she was in no mood to co-operate. It might be too easy for him to extract something she would hate him to know about.

'I don't think I'll bother going out today, thank you,' she said primly.

'It's an order, Miss Brown,' he said coldly, staring back at her, his mouth tight. 'I put it diplomatically, but since you don't choose to accept in the same light, you leave me no option but to remind you who's boss.'

He might be boss and she had to obey him, at least in working hours, but she wished he would maintain an appropriate distance between them. As they left the building he actually took her arm again as they crossed the foyer and, as before, she was forced to endure the many curious glances directed at them. She almost boiled with rage and despair when, as though to further the impression of intimacy, he bent down to murmur something, almost against her cheek.

'Just what do you think you're playing at!' she muttered between clenched teeth as their chauffeur driven car drove away and she rubbed the wrist he had refused to relinquish a few minutes earlier. 'First you're hanging on to Miss Veiga, now me!'

Nik laughed, leaning back, relaxed, regarding her flushed cheeks with cynical amusement. 'Aren't you getting things the wrong way round, Vicky?'

She started, then paled, her dark blue eyes widening as she thought quickly. Of course! As usual he was right. It had been her, but now Miss Veiga held pride of place. 'Miss Veiga is welcome to you!' she replied sharply, pain shooting through her.

'According to you, all women are,' he retorted mockingly.

'You have plenty.'

He said something under his breath in Greek which she didn't recognise but realised wasn't flattering. Let him curse—he couldn't hurt her more, she decided, not even if he beat her black and blue!

He took her to a famous restaurant in Curzon Street when she thought a much more modest one would have done. He plied her with wine and extravagant dishes until he got out of her, almost verbatim, everything Veiga had said the night before. She knew what he was doing, but anything more than one glass of wine always went to her head and she couldn't stop herself.

'Mr Veiga really likes the idea of you taking over,' she smiled. 'On condition.'

'I understand the conditions,' Nik drawled.

They had brandy with their coffee, and a rosy glow blotted out the misery in Vicky's heart. She was able to ask, with scarcely a twinge of pain, 'Are you going to marry her?'

'A man has to marry some time.' He stared at Vicky closely. 'I've been thinking about it for a while.'

'Then you'd better stop holding my hand in public, hadn't you?' she glanced down at their fingers, which were somehow entwined, with a wine-induced giggle. 'Mr Veiga mightn't like it!'

'It's a thought,' he agreed blandly, returning her to the office.

All sorts of rumours circulated during the next few days, most of which Vicky steadily ignored. Nik had been in New York for several days. He had gone alone, but someone had supposedly seen him there with the Veigas. When he came back he didn't say anything, but Vicky knew he was still seeing a lot of the Veigas. This was as much as she knew, though. Neither Gordon or she had heard anything definite about a take-over, although Gordon said this wasn't surprising as Nik often liked to have everything cut and dried before he said anything,

Vicky, while waiting for definite news in a state of numb resignation, set about doing something she realised she should have done when she had first returned from Greece. She saw an estate agent and asked them to sell her father's house. On their second day in Corfu, when she and Nik had gone to lunch with his aunt and uncle, his aunt had told her afterwards that Vera had paid nothing back. Minta Demetrious

hadn't blamed Vicky in any way, but she had wept
about it. They had been alone together for a short time
and she had related the whole sad story. Vera had
treated them disgracefully and taken most of their life
savings, some of which at least Vicky was determined to
repay.

The estate agent assured her the house should sell
well as it was in a good district and in excellent order.
He asked for a key and permission to show prospective
buyers over it and said he had several clients very
interested in this kind of property. In view of the
prospects of an early sale, Vicky began looking for
somewhere else to live, but on the low sum she allowed
herself she soon realised it wasn't going to be easy. She
tramped many miles and wasted a lot of time without
success.

Then, on top of that, just when she was already
feeling incredibly depressed, she and Nik quarrelled
unexpectedly. He came late to the office one afternoon,
looking remarkably pleased with himself.

Gordon had already left to keep an early evening
appointment and she was busy tidying her desk prior to
leaving herself. 'Good news?' she asked, glancing up at
Nik without thinking.

'Yes.' He sat down, then leaned forward, watching
her. 'I think so.'

Suddenly she went very cold. 'Veiga?'

'How did you guess?' he asked silkily, as if he had
known she'd thought of nothing else for days.

'He's agreed to sell?'

'Almost.' Nik ran a thoughtful hand around the back
of his neck. 'I believe I have persuaded him.'

His words almost flattened her, but with a desperate
endeavour she held on to her poise. 'And his daughter?'

Nik laughed. 'Don't worry, I'll soon rid him of that
little notion. Veiga doesn't realise it yet, but I have no
intention of marrying his daughter.'

Vicky stared at him. 'But you encouraged her!'

Complacently his mouth curled at the corners. 'I had to open the door for negotiations somehow.'

Vicky's cheeks stained with anger while her lips flew apart. 'Even if it means cheating?'

He didn't like that, she could tell. His grey eyes glittered, but she had no intention of apologising. She had been a fool to think he was capable of loving anyone; he was completely heartless! If she had thought about it sooner, she might have saved herself a lot of anguish.

Tears of humiliation sprang to her eyes, almost blinding her, so she didn't see the glitter in his eyes turn to fury, which might have prepared her for his savage attack.

'I don't have a monopoly on cheating, you know. Your own family would take some beating! Didn't your mother cheat my uncle out of nearly everything he had?'

'She's my stepmother,' Vicky gasped.

His voice seared her like a branding iron. 'What's the difference? You must have been partly responsible for her being the way she is. A carping, criticising stepdaughter is probably enough to drive anyone wrong in their mind!'

Vicky felt so wounded she almost cried out. 'I didn't criticise,' she whispered hoarsely, her face white.

'You never stop, with me!' he retorted furiously. 'You're always looking for perfection. Well, let me tell you, you won't find it. You'll still be looking for the perfect man in your lonely old age.'

Suddenly Vicky was furious too. 'It's surely not wrong to expect honesty, integrity! You'd almost sell your soul, Nik, to swell your already swollen empire. It's getting to be a fever in your blood you can't do without. You don't care who you trample over to add another successful take-over to your scalps!'

He gazed at her, his eyes stony and uncompromising. 'At least it ensures I have enough to pay my debts, both for myself and my family. In Greece we don't isolate ourselves from family commitments.'

'I'm going to sell the house!' she cried impulsively, his contempt forcing her to reveal what she had never intended to tell him.

'Why?' he asked sharply, clearly surprised.

'To repay your uncle.' There might be other reasons why such a sale was necessary, but they wouldn't benefit from it financially.

'You're mad!'

As well as carping and criticising! Vicky clasped her hands behind her back to stop them shaking. 'I realise I won't get as much as Vera took, but I will pay off the rest eventually.'

'How?'

'From my salary. After,' her voice faltered humiliatingly, 'after I leave you I'll find another job.'

'You can do what you like with your salary,' his teeth snapped together, 'but I refuse to let you sell your home.'

She didn't say it was already being advertised. 'A few weeks ago you threatened to sell it yourself.'

'My word!' Nik bit out. 'Do you remember everything? That was before I learned certain facts.'

'You mean that was before you believed me,' Vicky almost laughed. 'Anyway, you can't dictate what I do any longer—outside this office, that is.'

'You don't have to try and be tactful, Miss Brown,' he snapped harshly. 'Why don't you just spell it out without the wrappings? You mean I bully people and have no part in your personal life any more.'

'You couldn't spare the time, even if I wanted you. Which I don't!' she added hurriedly, glaring at him.

'Don't you?' he snarled, anger in every inch of him as he jumped up and came to her, dragging her to her feet. His eyes glittered ruthlessly down into hers as he stilled her struggles. 'You throw out challenges constantly.'

'No, I don't!' she gasped as the force of his fury whipped her like a storm. 'If I did,' she spluttered, 'you're quite capable of ignoring anything you don't want to see, but you enjoy tormenting me.'

'As much as you enjoy insulting me!' His voice had a furious ring to it as he pulled her suddenly right into his arms.

His kiss was an insult, searing right through her. He had no compunction about hurting her. There was no tenderness in it, just a desire to teach a lesson she would never forget. Rejection wasn't a word he either liked or understood, and he punished her savagely for it. His hands hurt almost as much as his mouth as they slid round her back to grip her soft flesh, and she felt the strong muscles of his arms binding her to him.

His kisses had a driving intensity which rapidly deprived her of breath, but when she tried to resist she felt her body slowly give to the hardness of his. The office faded as his embrace tightened and passion spiralled with a devastating wildness through her nerve centres. Helplessly her arms stole round his neck, her fingers burying themselves in the thick darkness of his hair, as beneath his plundering mouth, her own trembled in unmistakable surrender.

The ringing of the telephone became strident before Nik took any notice. Only slowly did he put Vicky from him to answer it. His breathing was deep and harsh and through glazed eyes she noticed his hand shaking as he brushed back his hair.

'I wonder how many such pleasurable interludes this damn thing interrupts?' he muttered sarcastically.

Vicky stared at him aghast, unable to move. She watched him pick up the receiver and begin talking to the caller, a concentrating frown on his face. It wasn't until she heard him laugh and say 'Rita' that she became aware that he must be talking to Miss Veiga, or someone who knew her.

The mention of Rita's name seemed to release Vicky

from the trance she was in. Swiftly picking up her handbag, she almost ran from the room.

'Vicky!' Nik suddenly slammed down the phone to come after her. 'Wait!'

At the door she paused so abruptly he nearly crashed into her. She was startled to see how pale he was. Had Rita had bad news? 'Don't let me interrupt you,' she muttered through bruised lips. 'You and I don't have anything more to say to each other.'

Nik stopped in his tracks, a curious greyness creeping under his skin. 'Can you honestly say that after the way you just kissed me?'

'That was merely physical,' Vicky whispered, flushing with shame.

'You don't care any more for me?'

Fiercely she shook her head, wanting above all things to believe it. 'I don't care for your opinion of me either! You make me hate you.'

His former anger seemed to fall from him like a cloak. He sounded almost pleading—or as near to it as he would ever get, she thought. 'I could change that, if you would let me,' he muttered.

'Only if you changed,' she breathed, knowing this was impossible.

'We could live together.' His eyes were suddenly violent, hiding the trace of desperation his voice betrayed. 'Then it wouldn't matter. You could have everything you want . . .'

'We've been through all this before,' she cut in, blinking angry tears from her eyes. In another minute she feared she might be ill. 'Do I have to keep on telling you I won't be bought?'

She had expected a scathing reply, but he simply blanched and stared at her. For a long, bitter moment they stared at each other until Vicky found the presence of mind to turn away. Afterwards she wasn't sure if she said goodnight, but Nik made no attempt to follow her.

When she reached home, Vicky was so exhausted she

was almost overcome with gratitude when Mrs Younger rang, inviting her to dinner.

'Your estate agent has been in and out all day with prospective buyers,' she said, 'and there might be more this evening, so if you come to me you will at least have your dinner in peace.'

Vicky didn't feel hungry so much as unable to face her own company, not after her latest session with Nik! The tension between them was getting to an intolerable pitch and she didn't see how she could go on working for him. If he was determined to have her for a mistress, she wondered how long she would be able to resist him. She had little faith in her ability to keep him at a distance if he really set out to wear her down.

He had said he had no intention of marrying Miss Veiga, but he might easily change his mind. He seemed able to sweep women in and out of his life like so much sawdust, but one day she feared he might meet someone who would come to matter more to him than any of the others. When this happened, Vicky knew she didn't want to be around. In her mind she was carefully wording her letter of resignation as she automatically washed her hands before going next door.

Mrs Younger had prepared a delicious meal which, despite her sore heart, Vicky enjoyed. After they finished Vicky made her go and sit in the lounge while she made coffee. When she returned with it, Mrs Younger told her there'd been a man at Vicky's front door.

'It looked like your boss, your ex-fiancé,' she said, deliberately lightly. 'Do you want to go and see?'

'No!' Vicky was so startled she almost dropped the tray she was carrying. 'If you don't mind, I'd rather not.'

Her expression, more than her words, sharpened Mrs Younger's attention. 'Have you quarrelled with him again?' she asked frankly. 'He did seem rather grim, and you were engaged.'

'In a way,' Vicky confessed reluctantly, praying her cheeks wouldn't go pink. 'We don't always get on.'

'I must say,' Mrs Younger remarked almost idly, 'it's not usual for a man in his position to bother about the feelings of his staff.'

Vicky was very fond of Mrs Younger and they had always been good friends. Because of this she forgave what she recognised as devious probing. She was quite right, of course, although men did sometimes get involved with their secretaries. But that didn't happen nearly as frequently as people were apt to believe, and a man in Nik's position, and with his looks, usually knew too many beautiful women to have to resort to chasing his office staff.

'He probably only wanted to see me about some minor detail which can wait until morning,' she shrugged, 'It can't be anything important or I wouldn't have forgotten.'

'Well,' Mrs Younger laughed, 'you can always say you weren't at home, if it was him. You wouldn't be telling a lie. Tell me,' she added, with a wry quirk at her own curiosity, 'is Mr Demetrious different to work for from the average Englishman?'

'Sometimes he seems more English than your average Englishman,' Vicky told her with a fierceness she wasn't aware of but which made Mrs Younger glance at her keenly again. 'Occasionally, though,' she frowned, unconsciously thoughtful, 'he is different—more assertive, and likes his own way.'

'With women . . .?'

Mrs Younger's soft interjection merely prompted Vicky's introspective thoughts. For a moment she forgot she was speaking aloud. 'Oh, yes,' she nodded. 'He thinks we should obey his every command. He wouldn't allow a girl to have an independent bone in her body if he had his own way. All he wants is humble, worshipping adoration.'

'Amounting to subservience?'

Suddenly realising how much she had been rambling on, and how indiscreetly, Vicky blushed scarlet. Hastily getting to her feet, she prepared to leave. 'It's just how he's made,' she stammered, 'but on the whole he's not too bad.'

'None of us are, all the time, thank goodness,' Mrs Younger observed lightly, drawing her own conclusions from the hectic colour in Vicky's cheeks. 'I still think it's a pity you decided not to marry him, though.' As Vicky gave a rather forced smile and said she must be going, Mrs Younger advised, 'Hadn't you better go out the back way, dear, for fear he's still there? You never know, he might be.'

Because she certainly didn't want to risk running into him, Vicky did go out the back way, but there was no sign of him. She decided that Mrs Younger had made a mistake, or he hadn't waited long. Recalling how they had parted, the coldness of his eyes, the bitter twist to his mouth, she couldn't imagine there had been anything important enough to make him want to see her again in a hurry.

Restlessly she searched in her handbag for the address of a small one-roomed flat a friend at work had given her. She was tempted to go and look at it straight away, it wasn't late. Then she realised how tired she was and knew it wasn't such a good idea. She had been up early that morning in order to leave everything tidy for the estate agent, and it would probably do her more good to have a bath and get into something cooler. The worrying business of finding somewhere to live would have to wait.

She was just coming from the kitchen, having filled the kettle in readiness to make herself a cup of tea later on, when the doorbell rang. Prickling all over with apprehension, she told herself it couldn't possibly be Nik. And, if it was, wasn't she crazy to imagine she couldn't face him when she might have to every day for several more weeks?

It wasn't Nik, however, when she eventually managed to force herself to go and see. It was some more people to look over the house. She was so relieved she smiled warmly and said it didn't matter when Mr Warren, the agent, apologised for disturbing her. Vicky did, in fact, welcome the interruption, feeling perhaps it was the diversion she needed.

This time the people viewing were a young professional couple who seemed very interested. They were obviously very much in love, and Vicky felt her heart almost ache with envy when the girl blushed and confessed that if they bought the house it would be their first home. As the agent was there it wasn't absolutely necessary for Vicky to go around with them, but as she had never sold a house before she was curious. She was also surprised to find she wasn't overwhelmed by the despair that often overtakes those who have to sell their homes. She frowned as she thought about it. This might be because she hadn't lived here for some years, or it could be that after Vera had come it had ceased to be a real home any more. It was only in her father's study that she felt a deep pang of nostalgia as she recalled the hours she had spent here with him in her childhood, talking and reading. Staring at his chair, she didn't like to think of someone else sitting there and her eyes misted. Quickly she averted her glance to the booklined walls, noting unhappily the wide, empty spaces. Vera had sold all the valuable editions, including some of the books Vicky had loved most of all.

When the young couple left they were very enthusiastic about the house, and Vicky thought she might have a word with Mr Warren tomorrow and ask if they had put a bid in for it. If they did, she might ask the agent to regard their offer favourably as she knew she would like them to have it.

It seemed quiet after they had gone and a feeling of loneliness, which she had never been conscious of before, made her think unhappily of the years ahead.

Marriage and children she must discount for ever, for there could never be anyone for her after Nik.

Tears ran down Vicky's cheeks as she took her shower, and, as she watched them drain away with the water, she wished she could get rid of her unhappiness as easily. Tears might give a kind of relief, but they rarely solved the underlying problem. It was no use trying to fool herself that she didn't love Nik to distraction. She had fought it, and for a short time she had believed she had succeeded, but she recognised now that the shock of discovering Nik's real plans, and her broken engagement, had merely frozen her feelings, not cured them. This evening, when he had been so furious with her, then invited her insultingly to live with him, the ice encasing her heart had cracked, revealing a torment which could only spring from unrequited love.

Slowly Vicky dried herself, then stepped on the bathroom scales before reaching for her thin robe. She was losing weight, the narrow cord would go round her waist twice, and the scales confirmed it.

With a sigh she remembered Nik's hands on her waist, lifting her against him as he had kissed her. Involuntarily she quivered. He enjoyed being cruel to her, he didn't pretend otherwise. It probably gave him a kind of sadistic satisfaction to wring a response from her when she refused to have anything to do with his questionable suggestions. Yet with Rita Veiga so obviously willing to entertain him, what could he want with an affair with his secretary?

The sickening feeling Vicky was experiencing increased as she went back to her bedroom. She suspected—and grew cold with the thought—that all he really wanted was to hear her say yes, then he would laugh in her face. On Corfu when she had refused to live with him this had hurt his pride and a thirst for revenge had to be assuaged. Just to hear her capitulate might be enough, and with a smothered groan of despair she wondered if he meant to continue pressurising her until she did.

Despite the warmth of the late summer evening, Vicky felt very cold as she went downstairs again to make her cup of tea. While the kettle boiled she got out a cup and found a teabag, then poured the boiling water over it. Such ordinary tasks did much to restore her normal composure. She even searched for a biscuit, although when she found it she knew she wouldn't be able to eat it and gave it instead to the few sparrows which frequently haunted her doorstep for titbits. She watched for a moment as they squabbled over it and bent down to crumble it in small pieces. Then, after washing her dusty hands, she picked up her cup and carried it to the lounge, where she decided she would read for a while before going to bed. If she went too early she might never sleep.

Deciding to read was one thing, concentrating on a book quite another. Eventually she gave up with a sigh and simply let her thoughts wander. There would be the contents of the house to dispose of, as well as the house itself. The agent had mentioned that if whoever bought the property didn't want the furniture it should be easy enough to sell, so that should be no problem. Vera had taken everything worth very much and there were only a few items Vicky would keep for herself. She couldn't take much to a one-roomed flat, and what she did need she would sort out that weekend.

Because she refused to allow herself to think of Nik but concentrated on other things, she was just beginning to sink into a state of dull lethargy when the bell rang again. As startled as she had been over an hour ago when it rang, she couldn't think who it could be. Mr Warren had said nothing about bringing another client this evening, so she ruled out that possibility.

When it suddenly struck her that it might be Nik, Vicky stumbled to her feet in fright, but after almost running to the hall she paused. She couldn't remember if the front door was locked, but if it wasn't, if it was

Nik, he surely wouldn't try it? The columned portico outside the door was deep. There was no way she could see who was outside by looking through a window. While she hesitated, her heart throbbing uneasily, to her utter amazement the door opened and her stepmother walked in.

Vera was the last person Vicky had expected to see. For weeks after Vera left she wondered what had happened to her, but she had been gradually forgetting about her when the Demetrious affair had restored her dramatically to Vicky's thoughts again.

Vera was that kind of person, Vicky realised, staring at her apprehensively as the first numbness of complete shock wore off. Nothing she ever did had a comforting ordinariness about it. From the day she had entered the house she had been a disturbing factor. And her irrational ways had brought Vicky's father a lot of misery, although Vicky was sure he had loved her.

'Well, well, well!' Vera had the soft, purring voice of a cat when something pleased her, but like a cat she could become sharp in an instant. She glanced at Vicky insolently. 'How nice to see you, but I should have guessed you'd be here. I might have known you'd be in the back door almost before I was out through the front!'

Mutely, while trying to find her tongue, Vicky shook her head. She wasn't quite sure what Vera meant and she didn't much care.

'What's the matter?' Vera's eyes narrowed as she watched Vicky's white face. 'You never had much to say for yourself, but I can't remember you being as silent as this.'

At last Vicky managed to speak. 'Why have you come back?' she whispered hoarsely.

'Not to hear you say how lovely it is to see you again, my darling stepmother,' Vera sneered. 'I'd be very disappointed if I'd been expecting a welcome like that!'

Meeting the cold dislike in her eyes, Vicky shivered.

'What would be the sense in pretending, either of us?'
she retorted bleakly.

'Darling, I never pretended anything,' said Vera with
sharp, amused sarcasm, removing the smart hat from
her head and tossing it carelessly on the hallstand. 'I'm
just trying to be civil.'

Vicky stared at her stepmother anxiously, wondering
what to do next. Vera didn't seem to have changed
much. She was as blonde as ever and as thickly made
up, so it was difficult to tell. The petulant droop of
her scarlet mouth was still there and discontent still
frowned from her brown eyes, but she was as
beautiful as she had always been. Vicky could
understand how Philip Demetrious had become in-
fatuated with her.

As though she were the hostess, not the visitor, Vera
walked straight past Vicky into the lounge, flinging
herself on the sofa. 'I'm thirsty,' she snapped, looking
pointedly at Vicky as she followed.

'I've made some tea.'

'Well! I haven't come down to that yet,' Vera
snapped. 'Haven't you anything stronger?'

Vicky took a deep breath. 'Half a bottle of sherry and
the same of whisky, which I believe you left.'

'Good grief!' Vera exclaimed in disgust. 'How do you
live? What do you give your friends?'

'They're usually quite happy with coffee.'

'Well, I'm not,' Vera retorted sharply. 'You can pour
me a large whisky.'

Vicky almost told her to get it herself, but that might
make Vera feel too much at home and all Vicky wanted
was to get rid of her. While she found a glass and
poured Vera a drink she heard her remark, 'Tea and
coffee would suit your friends, I suppose they're the
same dull lot. If you have a boy-friend I expect he
conforms to the same pattern.'

'I don't have a boy-friend,' Vicky said tersely.

'That's not surprising.' Vera tossed back her drink as

if it was water. 'You were always a prim little thing, you'd never find a man to suit you.'

Vicky felt a surge of relief that Vera had obviously not heard about Nik and she suddenly decided not to mention either him or his uncle. It would only amuse Vera to know she had caused such a upheaval. She would enjoy hearing how Philip Demetrious had gone almost crazy and she would never agree to repay the money she had taken. The sooner she got her out the house the better. When Vera came back—if ever she did, the house would be sold and she would tell Mrs Younger not to give her her new address.

'Where are you living now?' she asked, again wondering why Vera had paid her this visit.

'I was in a hotel,' Vera shrugged, 'until my money ran out.'

'Your money ran out?' Vicky repeated stupidly. 'I thought—that is, you hinted that your new husband was a millionaire.'

'I didn't get married again,' Vera replied flatly. 'It didn't work out.'

'You—you've just been living with him?' Vicky stammered incredulously.

'I did, for a few weeks,' Vera admitted carelessly. 'Now I'm broke, and I'm back.'

'Back?' all at once Vicky felt terribly apprehensive, 'Back where?'

'Here, of course,' Vera snapped belligerently. 'To this house. Where did you think? It's still mine, isn't it!'

CHAPTER TEN

VICKY gazed at her stepmother with horror in her eyes while a dreadful coldness came over her. 'You can't come back here to live,' she gasped. 'I'm busy selling the house!'

For a moment Vera looked furiously angry then she laughed. 'I'm afraid you can't. It's not already gone, is it?' she asked sharply.

'Not yet.'

Vera's eyes rested on Vicky's distressed face indifferently. 'Your father's will made it very clear that the house is mine until I remarry. As I haven't, the house isn't yours to sell.'

'But you left. You were so sure of getting married you sent me the key,' Vicky whispered suspiciously.

'I was getting married the next day,' Vera retorted bitterly, 'then he found out something about me and changed his mind. I could have sued him, but I didn't want the publicity.'

Vicky wondered, just as bitterly, if that was the real reason. The cards must have been heavily stacked against Vera to make her hesitate over taking such action.

'You never liked living here,' she said, hoping to dissuade her.

'True,' Vera shrugged contemptuously, 'but I do like a roof over my head.'

Vicky's legs suddenly gave way and she sank down in the nearest chair. She didn't know what to think, her mind seemed to be in a whirl. She would like to have asked Vera about the money she had taken from Philip Demetrious; she wanted to confront her about the pain she had caused him which had driven him to almost

168

taking his own life, and about using Vicky's name, but
something stopped her in time. If Vera hadn't married
again the house must still be legally hers, as she said,
and Vicky couldn't sell it. And if she told her she knew
all about Philip Demetrious, Vera would merely crow.
She would consider it a feather in her cap that a man
had gone even temporarily berserk over her. She
wouldn't believe it had been more a case of hurt pride
and that Philip had soon come to his senses. If she
learned that he had been in such a state, she might even
have the nerve to go and try and get more money out of
him, and while Vicky didn't imagine she would succeed,
she couldn't bear to think of the further pain this might
cause him—or to contemplate Nik's fury!

The more she thought of it, the more Vicky became
convinced she must be very careful if she hoped to
survive at all. At all costs she must protect Philip
Demetrious, but by doing so she might easily incur
Nik's wrath, to say nothing of Vera's!

'You must have been living on something,' she
muttered, trying to give herself more time to think.

'Oh, I had a stroke of good luck at roulette,' Vera
replied quickly and, Vicky guessed, untruthfully.

'If you intend staying I'll leave,' she said tensely.

'Why, there's no need for that,' Vera protested,
almost coaxingly. 'A house this size takes quite a bit of
keeping up. We could share the expenses.'

How did Vera intend paying her share with no money
or job? Vicky was about to ask, when again caution
warned her. It might save a lot of painful friction if she
pretended to go along with Vera's suggestion until she
found somewhere else to live. Then she could simply
disappear. Vera would never dare approach Nik to try
and discover where she was, but Vicky suspected that
once she had gone, Vera would forget all about her. No
doubt she would soon find another man to provide the
cash she seemed so badly in need of.

Curtly she nodded. 'As I gave up my flat I suppose

I'll have to stay.' She didn't miss the glint of satisfaction in Vera's small brown eyes.

Vicky was late for work next morning because she tried to contact the estate agent before she left. At such an early hour she wasn't able to get hold of anyone and had to wait until she reached the office. She didn't relish the task as, apart from anything else, she guessed the fees he would be entitled to for advertising alone might take most of her small savings.

Wearily she wished she hadn't mentioned anything to Nik about selling the house. He had told her not to and she had refused to listen, but she couldn't help wondering what his attitude would be when he heard she had taken it off the market. She had a feeling, for all the advice he had proffered, that he would admire her less.

As she hung up her jacket and tried to restore some order to her windblown hair, Vicky knew she couldn't explain about Vera. If she did she felt certain Nik would go immediately and see her and that somehow his uncle might get to know, and in Vicky's overwrought state it seemed imperative that she kept Nik and Vera apart.

When she rang the estate agent, as she had feared, he told her there would be certain fees to pay. She had no sooner put down the receiver than Vera rang. She had given Vera her extension number, hoping this might prevent her discovering she was the chairman's secretary, but she hadn't expected her to use it so soon.

'Why on earth did you go off without so much as fetching me a cup of tea?' Vera complained fretfully. 'I've been looking for you everywhere!'

'Was that all you called to tell me?' Vicky asked quickly. 'I've a lot to do, and I'm late as it is.'

'I had to make sure you weren't running away,' Vera said resentfully. 'I'm pretty broke and there's not much in the fridge—or anywhere, as far as I can see. You'd better do some shopping for dinner before you come home. And make sure you do—come home, I mean.'

'You can stop worrying,' Vicky even managed to sound faintly amused as well as reassuring, 'I'll live with you if you want me to, but I must go now. I'll see you later.'

As she turned from the telephone, she became aware of Nik standing in the doorway watching her, his face pale and coldly angry.

'You're late,' he snapped. 'Had a busy night?'

The sheer insolence in his voice set Vicky's teeth on edge. She hadn't realised he was in, and as she was late he was within his rights in complaining, but surely he could do it in a civilised manner?

'I'm sorry,' she apologised shortly. 'I slept in.'

This seemed to infuriate him to the point of violence and she wished apprehensively that she could have explained how late it had been before she had finished helping Vera with her unpacking, which her stepmother declared couldn't wait until morning. 'I was busy,' she confirmed quickly, wondering if Nik intended hitting her.

'Too busy to answer the door when I called to see you?' he rasped, entering her office and slamming the door so it nearly left its hinges.

'It must have been while I was having dinner with Mrs Younger,' she stammered. She said nothing about Mrs Younger thinking she had seen him. That would simply be asking for trouble!

'I don't believe you,' he replied flatly, his grey eyes impaling her nervous blue ones with glittering derision.

She was so distraught she almost said, 'Suit yourself,' but swallowed back the words in time. If his fury had any more fuel to feed on it might get completely out of control. Vicky didn't know why he should look ready to burst a blood vessel any moment. Surely being five minutes late and failing to answer the door weren't the greatest of crimes?

Taking a deep breath, Vicky replied with a calmness she didn't feel. 'You can always check, Mr Demetrious, and I am usually available.'

She had been going to add, in office hours, but
decided to let him work that out for himself. She wasn't
prepared for his mouth to curl quite so contemptuously
as he sneered, 'Really! Clive rang ten minutes ago and I
told him you weren't. It seems I made a mistake.'

Vicky bristled. 'You had no right to be so high-
handed!' she glared indignantly. 'You could at least be
polite to my friends!'

'I don't admire your choice of them,' he glared back
tightly, 'but Clive obviously didn't take any notice. You
were speaking to him just now.'

Vicky gasped, too confused to answer immediately.
Then she nodded, relieved that she hadn't denied it.
Perhaps it was better that he should believe she had
been talking to anyone but Vera.

Nik caught her arm in such a fierce grip it sent fear
burning along her nerve ends, and a gasp of shock
escaped her as his eyes seemed to turn black. 'So,' he
snarled, 'you've given in at last. May I be the first to
wish you joy of each other.'

'What are you talking about?' she whispered.

'You said you would live with him.'

He had overheard! Vicky's face went white as she
realised she was trapped by her own folly, by her desire
to save both Nik and his uncle more pain. But did it
really matter what she did? Nik wanted nothing more to
do with her. So whatever she did couldn't matter any
more.

'I'm thinking about it,' she managed to reply, almost
idly.

'That wasn't thinking about anything,' he said
savagely. 'That was total commitment.'

Deliberately Vicky shrugged, but fortunately, just as
she feared Nik was going to strike her, Gordon
appeared.

The day dragged, with Nik in such a foul temper that
even Gordon, who could usually cope with his moods,
did his best to keep out of his way. Nik kept up a

stream of continuous criticism until Vicky could
sometimes have burst into tears. It was after six before
she was able to leave and she had a feeling that he
would liked to have kept her at the office all night.

On her way home she bought some cooked meat and
salad as there wouldn't be time to cook a hot meal.
Most of the shops she usually went to were closed, but
as long as she had something, she reasoned, Vera
couldn't very well demand to be taken out for dinner.

Vera was furious because it was seven before Vicky
got in. Obviously the sight of Vicky laden with
purchases must have made her feel confident she
wouldn't desert her in a hurry.

'I'm starving,' she snapped, almost before Vicky was
through the door. 'Where've you been?'

'Working,' Vicky replied dryly.

'I realise,' Vera retorted sharply. 'After this, I think
you'll have to hand over your pay cheques to me. It
should be a help, when you're so busy, if I take charge
of the accounts.'

Vicky, having no intention of doing any such thing,
said coolly, 'You never liked shopping.'

'I can order by phone.' Vera slumped in a kitchen
chair and lit a cigarette.

There were two empty cartons on the table sporting
the name of a famous wine merchant. Vicky eyed them
resignedly as she dumped her parcel of groceries beside
them. 'I gather you've already ordered a supply of
drink. In my name, I presume?'

'I was sure you wouldn't mind, darling,' Vera blew
careless smoke rings. 'Think of the embarrassment of
not being able to offer anyone a drink!'

Vicky didn't reply as she began emptying the carrier
containing her shopping.

'I could do with some new clothes,' Vera said next,
watching Vicky but doing nothing to help. 'If I could
borrow some money or you could let me have a blank
cheque I could go tomorrow.'

Vicky glanced at her, feeling almost sick with despair. Vera would never change. She couldn't have forgotten the five suitcases full of expensive clothes Vicky had carried from the doorstep and unpacked for her the previous night. And while knowing Vicky had only the salary she worked for she would have no hesitation in buying a fresh supply of things she didn't really need. That was, if she could find someone foolish enough to give her carte blanche with their cheque book!

Mumbling something about having to see, Vicky set about preparing dinner. All the time she made the salad and heated soup, her mind was busier than her fingers. Vera never had enough money. She was happy enough spending it, but as soon as she realised Vicky had none she would resort to her usual methods of getting some, and these Vicky didn't care to contemplate. Suddenly she knew she couldn't stay here with Vera, not even for another night. As soon as dinner was over she would ring a hotel. There were one or two small ones in the vicinity who might have a room to spare; she would stay there. In a few days, with any luck, she might find a place of her own. Vera was welcome to the house. If it hadn't been for Philip Demetrious she would have no regrets, but it was no use hoping that Vera would ever consider she owed him anything, or attempt to pay him anything back.

The meal Vicky managed was appetising if ordinary, but she found she could scarcely eat a thing. She hadn't been able to eat any lunch either and knew she should be feeling hungry, but she was only able to swallow a little soup. Vera didn't appear to notice. After she finished she wandered off to the lounge without comment, other than to say she would like some coffee.

Vicky switched the percolator on, then hurriedly washed up, unwilling to leave an untidy kitchen. Then, while the coffee perked, she rang one of the hotels she had in mind and was relieved when they said they could take her. She couldn't be sure of the exact time, but she told them she should be there within the next hour or so.

Breathing a sigh of relief, Vicky returned to the kitchen to rinse her clammy hands and collect Vera's coffee. She had no idea Vera had listened to her phone call until she walked into the lounge and found her in a fuming temper. Vera began shouting so hard that neither of them heard the doorbell ring, or if they did it didn't register.

'Just where do you think you're going?' she flung at Vicky, almost before the girl was through the door. Following a lot of unrepeatable abuse, she exclaimed, 'I heard you on the phone. If you think you can run out on me you're mistaken!'

With a sinking heart, Vicky glanced at the half empty whisky bottle by her stepmother's side and realised Vera had been drinking. She had probably been drinking half the afternoon.

'You can't stop me.' She put down the tray she was carrying and gazed at her stepmother dully. 'I thought it would be easier for both of us if I just slipped out. I don't want to quarrel with you, Vera.'

'My girl!' Vera's voice was echoing and shrill. 'It's your duty to stay and look after me. You don't believe I'm going to let you walk out, just like that!'

'Oh, Vera,' Vicky could feel herself beginning to tremble, 'you know we have nothing in common.'

'That's true, anyway,' Vera raged, diverted. 'You were always a sanctimonious little thing, always looking down your nose at me!'

'That's not true,' Vicky denied.

'Don't contradict me!' Vera blazed. 'And you're staying!'

'Vera,' Vicky protested hoarsely, 'you know it won't be long before you find some man . . .'

'And why not?' Vera shrieked. 'You were always jealous of my ability to attract men, weren't you? At least I got plenty out of them to keep me in a way your mean old father never did.'

'He—he loved you, and he was your husband,' Vicky protested, completely stricken.

Vera ignored this. 'If you hadn't been so straitlaced you could have enjoyed yourself too. I'll never forget your face when you discovered me upstairs in bed with someone. How old were you then, seventeen?'

'Vera, please!'

Vera merely laughed cruelly. 'I've always been attractive to men. I still am, and it certainly pays off. Why, only this year, on Corfu . . .'

She paused as Vicky's eyes widened. She was sure Vera had been going to mention Philip Demetrious. 'What were you going to say?'

'It doesn't matter,' Vera muttered sullenly, ignoring the coffee she had demanded in favour of more whisky.

'I think it does!' a curt voice clipped behind them, causing them both to jump. Vicky was vaguely conscious of the bottle in Vera's hands dropping back on the table with a clatter as they both stared apprehensively at Nik Demetrious. The clattering seemed to increase wildly in Vicky's head until she felt almost deafened.

Vera's eyes were fixed nervously, though with growing appreciation on Nik's tall, impressive figure. She couldn't believe his ruthless expression had anything to do with her, and she was not one to let an opportunity slip. 'Who are you?' she asked, fluttering long, mascara-laden lashes at him.

Nik eyed her with contempt. 'My name happens to be Demetrious, Nik Demetrious. Perhaps it reminds you of someone?'

Vicky watched Vera's face go pale, then purple, an ugly colour which didn't exactly flatter her. It made her look older, suddenly revealing her for what she was. Shock eddying through Vicky, her glance returned to Nik. What was he doing here? How had he got in?

Without removing his eyes from Vera's face, he

addressed Vicky. 'Wait for me outside in the car, Vicky.' He threw her the keys.

'Why?' Vicky asked, her stomach lurching.

Nik's voice was tinged with anger and impatience and something else she couldn't so easily define. 'Just do as I say. Now!'

As she left he called after her, 'I'll join you in a minute, after I've had a word with your stepmother.'

Huddled in Nik's car, Vicky clutched her handbag tightly. When she realised what she was doing, she let it slide to the floor, wondering why she had unconsciously snatched it from the hall table. She wasn't going anywhere with Nik, of this she was certain. She was still resolved to leave and she would have to go back and pack her things, wouldn't she?

The last person she had expected to see was Nik. He hadn't said how he had got in. The door must have been open. Vera should really get it seen to. This could be the only explanation, but she hadn't dared ask him, because he'd looked so furious. Had he realised that Vera was the woman who had cheated his uncle on Corfu? If he had, what might he not do to her? Suddenly convulsed with fright, Vicky left the car to return to the house.

Nik almost knocked her over coming down the steps from it. Behind him she saw Vera rush across the hall and slam the door. At least she seemed still capable of doing that, Vicky thought, staring stupidly, with a strange kind of relief.

'Didn't I tell you to get in the car?' Without apology, Nik picked Vicky up, striding towards it. 'Ah, I see you obeyed me.' His eyes narrowed as he noticed her handbag. 'Why didn't you stay here?'

'I was frightened you might strangle her,' Vicky confessed, as he lowered her carefully to the passenger seat and got in beside her.

'It would have been no more than she deserved,' he said tersely. 'I didn't lay a finger on her, but I can assure you she won't ever bother you again.'

He fastened the seat belt over Vicky's slender body, his face momentarily remote, full of hard, angry lines.

Vicky swallowed and shivered as she lifted her head from watching, mesmerised, the gentle movements of his hands. 'I can't go with you. I've booked a room at the Riverton Hotel. I have my packing to do.'

'You have your handbag.'

'Yes.' She found it difficult to speak, her throat one big ache.

'That's all you need, then.' He ignored the protesting flutter of her hands with which she tried to be more explicit. Decisively he threw the car into action and roared off. 'We'll call at the Riverton, I believe I know where it is, and I'll cancel any bookings you've made. You're coming with me!'

'Nik . . .'

'Unless,' a hard jaw set squarely, 'you'd rather go to Clive?'

She stiffened. 'I wasn't even thinking of him, but that doesn't mean I'm willing to go with you.'

'You were talking to Clive this morning.'

'No, I wasn't.' Vicky wished she could get a better grip of herself so that her voice didn't feel like it was floating above her head. It seemed to be answering Nik's questions as if it were a part of her over which she had no control. 'I spoke to the estate agent, cancelling the sale of the house. As Vera didn't marry again, you see, the house is legally hers until she does, so it isn't mine to sell. Then she rang.'

Nik appeared to follow her fairly well and his voice reflected his fury. 'So it was she who wanted you to live with her? To run after her, I suppose, and provide for her until something better turned up? You were talking to her, not Clive, when I came in?'

Vicky nodded, though no more happily. 'You jumped to the wrong conclusions.'

'And you let me—and how I suffered for it!' she heard him mutter under his breath.

He pulled up so abruptly outside the Riverton that she was glad of her seatbelt. 'Shan't be a moment,' he said, frowning, as he paused, on her pale, apprehensive face. 'I should take you with me, just to make sure you don't run away, but you look as though even a few yards might be too much for you.'

'I'll be fine.' She watched him striding into the hotel wondering if she ever would be again. She knew a terrible compulsion to run, although she didn't know where she could run to. One by one every avenue of escape was being closed to her. She wondered where she could go after Nik had finished talking to her. Had he forgotten she must have somewhere to spend the night? She nerved herself to follow him, to cancel the cancellation, but before she could move he was back, and when she tried to tell him he had been too presumptuous, he told her roughly to shut up!

She was still trying to find the strength to fight him when they arrived at his penthouse.

'Whatever will Dion think?' she stammered, feeling a mass of raw emotion and suddenly bursting into tears.

'Vicky!' Nik reached her quickly, with strong arms to draw her to him. 'Don't be so distraught. If anyone has the right to be that, I think it must be me. I've been in hell all day, although it must have been my own fault,' he admitted grimly.

When she sniffed miserably and buried her wet face against him, he drew her gently but with determination from the car. 'Dion will be alarmed if I don't turn up for dinner,' he murmured teasingly. 'He will think something has happened to me.'

In the penthouse, in the lounge, he released her. Vicky didn't notice Dion hovering in the background until she heard Nik speaking to him. 'Leave dinner, Dion. You may take the rest of the evening off. Miss Vicky and I will help ourselves later. She will be staying.'

'Yes, *kyrie*.' Vicky saw Dion was smiling as he left them.

'I can't stay here!' she protested, as Dion closed the door behind him and Nik drew her down on the huge, silk-covered settee in the warm, quiet room.

'I hope you will,' he said simply, his eyes going swiftly over her tear-stained cheeks. 'I'm praying you will.' He rose again to pour two drinks and placed one in her hands. 'Drink it up,' his voice was commanding but anxious, 'you're in a state of shock.'

Vicky tried not to look at him sitting beside her. She just wished she could find a hole to crawl into and die. Suddenly she was aware that she was still wearing her office clothes, that her face must be bare of make-up, her hair untidy. 'Nik,' she whispered, trying to prevent more weak tears from falling, 'why did you come to the house this evening?'

His hands clenched as he appeared to restrain himself with a visible effort. 'I'll tell you after you drink your brandy,' he replied sternly, and watched while she did, until a little colour returned to her pale cheeks. Then he finished off his own drink in one gulp and turned to her, his face haggard, his grey eyes tormented, as if still comsumed by remembered pain.

'It was Clive. I believed he was there with you. I thought about it until I couldn't stand it any more. I had to see you together to know beyond doubt you were going to live with him. I realised if I found you with him I might go crazy. I was on the verge of it when I heard voices. I rang and then I decided to try the door. I'd never known what it was like before, wanting to kill a man. It took me a minute to realise you were talking to another woman, but it's a minute I have no wish to live through again.'

Vicky's mind was reeling, her heart coming alive again and thumping. 'You mean you actually cared that I might have been there with Clive?'

'I care.' His voice roughened thickly as he stared at

the silky head bending in flushed confusion. 'If I kissed you, my darling, you might realise how much, but I have to talk to you first. And I may not have the right to kiss you, after everything I've said and done.'

The pain in his voice was explicit. In startled wonderment, Vicky raised her drooping head to look at him. 'Are you trying to say you—you love me?' she stammered.

'Didn't you guess?' he groaned, flushing a dark red. 'I've been almost maniacal!'

'How could I,' she said huskily, 'after everything that happened? I thought you hated me. I know you asked me to marry you on Corfu, but I believed that was only because of your conscience, after you learned that you made a mistake about me.'

'In a way it was,' he confessed heavily, tension in every line of his powerful body. 'I was in a state of shock, for the first time in my life utterly confused by my own feelings. Apart from our mock engagement, as one might call it, I'd never asked a woman to marry me before. I would never admit it, but I knew when I asked you a second time it wasn't merely because of my conscience. When you refused I was furious. I told myself it was all for the best. I tried to convince myself I had done everything I could do. And it was only because my pride had suffered a setback that I couldn't forget you.'

Vicky stared at him in stupefied disbelief. 'Oh, Nik,' she whispered, 'I had no idea. Perhaps I was too busy guarding my own feelings to be able to judge yours. I'd loved you almost from the day I came to work for you. After I learned what Vera had done to your uncle I tried to make allowances for what you'd done to me, but I thought you'd killed my love. When I realised I still loved you as much as ever, you were involved with Rita Veiga and I didn't think I had a chance.'

'Vicky! Oh darling!' He suddenly caught her close, silencing her trembling lips with a kiss he couldn't seem to do without. 'I can't tell you how sorry I am. I didn't realise what a contemptible brute I was until you told me the truth about myself yesterday. I didn't even like Rita Veiga very much, yet I wasn't above using her in order to get hold of her father's business.'

'You sent her flowers,' Vicky reproached him, burying her hot face against his shoulder.

'If I hadn't been so uptight over you,' Nik murmured ruefully, 'I could have explained. She was our hostess at the party. The flowers were merely a courtesy gesture—the usual way of saying thank you.'

'I tried to believe that,' Vicky revealed, 'but I was so jealous!'

Nik kissed her again, his mouth growing increasingly passionate as she clung to him, then he withdrew on a long, hard breath, holding her with determination away from him. 'I've still some explaining to do.'

'It doesn't matter,' she whispered, only wanting to be in his arms. It was so wonderful to discover they loved each other that nothing else seemed to matter. 'In Greece you have different customs, Nik. I understand why you acted as you did.'

Smiling soberly, he shook his head. 'I admit I might have more of the old pagan blood of my ancestors in my veins than I thought, but when Philip nearly died, while there was anger in my heart, I had no real intention of seeking revenge. That didn't happen until later, when I discovered the girl who I believed to be the same one who had tricked Philip was still working for the firm.

'Such apparently diabolical nerve infuriated me to such an extent that I was determined to teach you a lesson you would never forget. At that stage, however, I didn't have a real plan. I did need a secretary, and when I was assured that you were bright and efficient I decided this might be one way of getting you in my clutches, so to speak, while I thought of something.

'You probably find it incredible that I could act in

such a way,' he went on grimly, 'but I was so angry about you that I think for a time I couldn't think straight. When I saw you standing in front of me, looking so young and innocent, something snapped. Something terrible seemed to be happening inside me. I thought it was hate, but I know now it was love. Something must have instinctively warned me, though, and at the time, it raised the devil in me, making me quite capable of the worst kind of violence.

'The first plot I conceived was fairly uncomplicated. To allow you the prestige of being my secretary at an increased salary, then, just as your confidence was soaring, to demand the money you had taken from Philip and dismiss you. I don't know when I thought of asking you to marry me or how I managed to be sufficiently convincing to carry it off.'

'If I hadn't been so much in love with you,' Vicky confessed, 'I might have realised something was very wrong. You didn't say you loved me, but every time I grew doubtful,' she admitted with a wry smile, 'I put it down to another of your Greek customs. I believed you mightn't speak of love until we were actually married.'

Without returning her slight smile, Nik shook his head. 'Each time I kissed you I became aware of your increasing attraction until in the end I scarcely dared touch you. Several times when I had you in my arms I almost lost control; you don't know what it cost me to let you go. Challenging you about Philip was one of the hardest things I'd ever done, the way I felt forced to break our engagement nearly killed me. It was only your regular protestations of innocence, which I disbelieved, that hardened me enough to stop me throwing myself at your feet and declaring that I didn't care what you had done.

'But despite that, and Corfu, and just about everything, I didn't realise exactly how much I loved you until you went for me about the Veigas yesterday. I felt sick to my very soul,' he said, his eyes dark, his face white, 'I just wanted to crawl out of sight. But today, when I thought I heard you promising to live with Clive, I really knew what it was like to suffer. I might detest your stepmother,' he added, 'but at least I was relieved to find her with you tonight and not Clive.'

Vicky swallowed. 'I'm sorry about Vera. I think she's spent all your uncle's money, and I won't be able to pay it back either.'

Nik shrugged. 'She's welcome to keep everything. It will be compensation enough not to see her again.' For a moment his eyes narrowed. 'I don't wish to seem curious, Vicky, but I couldn't help overhearing her remark about you finding her in bed with someone.'

Vicky hadn't realised this, and her face paled again as she tried haltingly to explain. 'Vera was very fond of giving parties, or going to them, almost every night. I usually stayed in my bedroom, and one evening while I was there, when she had guests, I heard a noise in the spare room next to mine and found her there with a strange man.'

Nik's face hardened with fury as he imagined the scene. 'That was obviously the reason why, at first anyway, you could scarcely bear me to touch you?'

'Yes,' Vicky admitted, beginning to tremble as words tumbled from her lips and she was unable to stop them. 'For years, as soon as any man got close I was panic-stricken. I couldn't seem to help it. It was a shock discovering Vera, but maybe nothing so terrible. I think it was what she said more than anything else. It left me with the impression that all sex was sordid, and no matter how I tried to reason with myself, I couldn't manage to get over it. It wasn't until I met you that anything changed—and then it wasn't much,' she confessed unevenly. 'But as soon as I realised I was falling in love with you everything looked different. Suddenly I wasn't frightened any more, I began to see things in their proper perspective. Until . . .'

As her voice trailed off unhappily, Nik's arms

tightened round her and some muttered words of self-depreciation escaped him. Yet as he drew her protectively closer and a little of his remorse got through to her, something inside her became wonderfully alive again and responding. She recognised with a kind of tumultuous gratitude that everything was going to be all right. No longer did Vera's actions have the power to disturb her. It might always disturb her in a way that there were those who lived by their wits, as Vera did, but the rules of morality were clearly defined, and people must have the right to choose for themselves.

She heard Nik saying heavily, 'It would seem that both your stepmother and myself have a lot to answer for. Do you think you will ever be able to love me again, Vicky, after all I've done?'

She lifted such a tearful but radiant face to him that his breath caught. 'I've never really stopped loving you,' she said tremulously.

'Darling!' For a long moment she thought he had stopped breathing, then she saw something move convulsively in his throat, and, as her heavy lashes fell, his mouth traced a path down her cheek until he worshipfully found her lips. As they clung together she felt in him a violent yet tender hunger, and as he strained her to him her body was consumed by leaping flames of delight. Desire raced through her veins, making her weak and vulnerable, but there was nothing frightening, only a deep yearning inside her to belong to him completely.

As if he, too, was consumed by the same depth of feeling, Nik muttered hoarsely against her soft mouth, 'How long before you will marry me? A week—two? Don't ask me to wait any longer, my little love, I want you so much.'

'Whenever you like,' Vicky whispered back, her fingers digging into his muscular shoulders. 'I feel the same way.'

'Wanton!' he teased, but there was humble relief in his eyes as they sobered. 'I love you, my darling. I don't care about the business. I'll still carry on, but I'll take more time off. You really opened my eyes to what rampant ambition can do to a man!'

'Oh, Nik,' she smiled mistily, drawing back a little, 'I don't condemn you for being ambitious.'

'I still am,' he smiled wryly, though his voice thickened, 'but in other directions. I want a wife, a proper home and a family.'

'A family?' Vicky blushed, her eyes shy but adoring. 'I'd like two girls and a boy.'

'Make it two boys and a girl, Miss Brown,' he laughed, then drew her back to him fiercely. 'I love you,' he repeated, as if he couldn't say it often enough, and with a smothered exclamation he suddenly picked her up and carried her through to his bedroom.

Laying her gently on the bed, he came down beside her and began kissing her passionately. 'I must have you to myself for another few minutes before dinner,' he murmured huskily, 'I hope you're not too hungry?'

She gave a little shaken sigh as his hand slipped under her blouse and closed her eyes as every touch, every caress, every kiss Nik gave her told of his growing need of her. 'I don't mind if we don't eat at all,' she whispered in reply, her cheeks on fire, her heart racing.

'I'm only hungry for you,' he muttered, his eyes darkening, a hectic flush on his cheekbones as he gazed at her. 'You don't know how much I want to make love to you!'

As his mouth crushed hers, a wonderful tenderness mingling with his passion, Vicky's lips parted beneath his in joyous response as her arms crept round his neck to draw him still closer. 'I don't want to wait any longer,' she murmured. 'Oh, Nik, I do love you!'

Her trust moved him visibly. His eyes blazed as his arms tightened. 'I won't ever let you out of my sight again, Vicky. I hope you realise you won't ever escape?'

'I won't ever want to,' she replied softly against his mouth, a raging fire inside her as her limbs began melting into his, as his hand slid across her stomach to curve over her hips.

'Darling,' he muttered, and her own reply was lost in the raging torrent of sensation that washed over them, sweeping them swiftly into paradise.

Harlequin Plus

A WORD ABOUT THE AUTHOR

Margaret Pargeter's earliest memories are of her childhood in Northumberland, in northern England. World War II was raging, but in spite of the gravity of the times, she recalls, people always tried to find something to smile about. That memory, and that philosophy, have stayed with her through the years.

Short-story writing was a habit that began in her early teens, and after her marriage she wrote serials for a newspaper. When her children were in school she did several years of market research, which she believes gave her a greater insight about people and their problems, insight that today helps her in creating interesting plots and developing believable characters.

Today, Margaret lives in a small house in the quiet Northumbrian valley where she grew up. On the subject of writing romances, she is convinced of one thing: "It is not easy. But not the least among my blessings is the pleasure I get from knowing that people enjoy reading my books."

ROBERTA LEIGH

A specially designed collection of six exciting love stories by one of the world's favorite romance writers—Roberta Leigh, author of more than 60 bestselling novels!

1 **Love in Store**

2 **Night of Love**

3 **Flower of the Desert**

4 **The Savage Aristocrat**

5 **The Facts of Love**

6 **Too Young to Love**

Available now wherever paperback books are sold, or available through Harlequin Reader Service. Simply complete and mail the coupon below.

Harlequin Reader Service

In the U.S.
P.O. Box 52040
Phoenix, AZ 85072-9988

In Canada
649 Ontario Street
Stratford, Ontario N5A 6W2

Please send me the following editions of the Harlequin Roberta Leigh Collector's Editions. I am enclosing my check or money order for $1.95 for each copy ordered, plus 75¢ to cover postage and handling.

☐ 1   ☐ 2   ☐ 3   ☐ 4   ☐ 5   ☐ 6

Number of books checked_____ @ $1.95 each = $_____

N.Y. state and Ariz. residents add appropriate sales tax $_____

Postage and handling $ .75

                                                   TOTAL $_____

I enclose_____

(Please send check or money order. We cannot be responsible for cash sent through the mail.) Price subject to change without notice.

NAME_____
                        (Please Print)
ADDRESS_____ APT. NO._____

CITY _____

STATE/PROV._____ ZIP/POSTAL CODE_____

Offer expires February 29, 1984   30856000000

RL-N

Take these 4 best-selling novels FREE

Yes! Four sophisticated, contemporary love stories by four world-famous authors of romance FREE, as your introduction to the Harlequin Presents subscription plan. Thrill to **Anne Mather**'s passionate story BORN OUT OF LOVE, set in the Caribbean.... Travel to darkest Africa in **Violet Winspear**'s TIME OF THE TEMPTRESS....Let **Charlotte Lamb** take you to the fascinating world of London's Fleet Street in MAN'S WORLD .... Discover beautiful Greece in **Sally Wentworth**'s moving romance SAY HELLO TO YESTERDAY.

The very finest in romance fiction

Join the millions of avid Harlequin readers all over the world who delight in the magic of a really exciting novel. EIGHT great NEW titles published EACH MONTH! Each month you will get to know exciting, interesting, true-to-life people . . . . You'll be swept to distant lands you've dreamed of visiting . . . . Intrigue, adventure, romance, and the destiny of many lives will thrill you through each Harlequin Presents novel.

Get all the latest books before they're sold out!
As a Harlequin subscriber you actually receive your personal copies of the latest Presents novels immediately after they come off the press, so you're sure of getting all 8 each month.

Cancel your subscription whenever you wish!
You don't have to buy any minimum number of books. Whenever you decide to stop your subscription just let us know and we'll cancel all further shipments.

Introducing...

Harlequin American Romance

An exciting new series of sensuous and emotional love stories—contemporary, engrossing and uniquely American. Long, satisfying novels of conflict and challenge, stories of modern men and women dealing with life and love in today's changing world.